To Betty + Etta —
Thanks! Enjoy!

DOUBLE STALK

by

Ann Snuggs

Ann Snuggs
June 2018

Copyright © 2013 Ann Snuggs

All Rights Reserved

Other than excerpts for review purposes, no portion of this book may be transmitted, entered or stored in a retrieval system, photocopied or reproduced in any way or by any means without written permission of the copyright holder.

This book is a work of fiction. Any resemblance to actual events or persons, living or dead, is entirely coincidental.

ISBN-13: 978-1484892985
ISBN-10: 1484892984

First edition

Cover design by Ann Snuggs

This one's for you, Todd.

ACKNOWLEDGEMENTS

Writing is a solitary pursuit yet few, if any, writers live in total isolation. Soon into this story, Ann Lightsey became an early reader. Other readers through the writing and editing process included Deborah Horn and Sue Winsor. I appreciate their help and support.

Thanks to Thomas Harwick for the help with formatting. One of these days my tech will catch up with my needs. Until then I'll be seeking his help for the final draft.

However, I owe the greatest debt for *Double Stalk* to Kristofer Todd Upjohn. In conversation concerning films of the early-to-mid-1990s, he made a casual comment that popped the premise of this tale into my mind. It was as if he had shown a spotlight on a completed outline. He critiqued each chapter as I worked and did a final edit before my "stalker novel," as I've always referred to it, was made available for public consumption. Without his input and support none of these characters would have ever come to life for me, as I hope they will for the reader.

Any e-publishing on my part must include a tip of the hat to Dr. Fred Zackel for his initial push to "just do it."

My deepest appreciation to all, named and unnamed, who have helped me so much.

PROLOGUE

"Damn!" Clint Sharkey hurled the magazine across the room. "Everyone is a critic! Here's some bitch in some hick town in the Midwest telling me how to make my movies. Five-to-one she's never seen even one of them. It's not enough that the half-assed politicians condemn things they've never seen or heard. Now every bitch on the street wants in on the act. This is nineteen ninety-five! In six more years we'll be in the twenty-first century. These hicks need to grow up!"

Pete Spencer laughed. "Remember, Clint, you like controversy. Isn't that what you said when the critics blasted our first production? Shove violence and obscenities right in their faces. Or was that the term you used?"

The writer-director grinned wryly. "You know damned well exactly what I said." He shrugged. "Just overreaction I guess. These right-wing hypocrites make me want to puke. They're so sure that they have all the answers; and too many of them are gaining power. Freedom of expression will be right out the window. And you know how I like to express myself," he finished with a twinkle in his eye.

"Your temper and I have certainly met. What did this one say?"

"That I need to improve my damn vocabulary."

Pete whooped with laughter. "I can't believe that set you off after some of the serious critics, people who count in the business, have said so much worse."

"At least most of them saw the damn films. It just pisses me off for someone to spout off about things they know nothing about."

"Maybe this bitch has seen your movies. Maybe she's some English teacher with a vocabulary hang-up. Did she really say 'damn'? Maybe she's a groupie trying to get your attention. Maybe . . ."

"Maybe you should keep your friggin' thoughts . . . . Hey, that's an idea. Maybe the magazine would give me her return address."

"What the hell are you planning, Clint? A confrontation by mail?"

A speculative gleam flickered in the director's eyes and a wicked smile touched his lips. "Not exactly. Picture this scenario. Not rabid fan stalks celebrity, but noted celebrity stalks non-fan. Interesting? Provocative? I like it."

"Get serious. This time you *have* slipped over the edge. Think of *these* headlines: 'Celeb Writer/Director Indicted.' Or better yet, 'Reverse Stalking Lands Director in Asylum.' Forget it."

"Good publicity. I'll write the script like a diary. My fans will eat it up."

Clint crossed the room, retrieved the discarded magazine and thumbed through it, searching for the masthead. "Aha, here's the phone number."

Ann Snuggs

Double Stalk

CHAPTER 1

In a city in the Midwest, Michelle Wilson inserted her mailbox key and braced herself for the barrage of junk mail that usually attacked her. The front swung open allowing two or three catalogs and a handful of envelopes to drop out. She caught them deftly and shuffled them into a neat stack. Once inside her apartment Michelle deposited the mail on the coffee table and headed to the bedroom to change into sweats.

"Sultan, where are you?" she called, stepping out of her skirt. "Sultan?"

A large, gray Persian cat crawled from under the bed and stretched leisurely. He sat down, curled his tail around his body and looked up at her with reproachful eyes.

"Yes, Your Majesty, I know I'm late. I was trying to close a deal so that you could have the finest cat food." Michelle leaned down to stroke the Persian. "Somebody around here has to make a living."

Sultan gave her a casual glance and stalked off into the living room. Michelle shook her head and laughed. Cats were such insolent animals.

After supper she gathered up the mail, which Sultan had nudged into the floor, and began the sorting process. Bills in one stack, money requests in another, catalogs and ads in still another. As she reached for the last ad, Michelle noticed a plain white envelope that had fallen from the stack. It rested under the far side of the coffee table. She leaned down and stretched to reach it.

"That's odd," she said to herself. "Most of these soliciting companies use some type of return address."

Michelle ripped open the envelope and a torn piece of paper fluttered out. Letters cut from a newspaper spelled, "Someone is watching you."

She dropped the missive as if it were a hot rock. Her next move was easily explainable, a quick glance to make sure the curtains were drawn. Michelle then took a deep breath and began to reason with the unreasonable fear that had suddenly possessed her.

"It's a prank," she told herself firmly. "Some competitor being childish about a missed sale. Some friend kidding her about her beloved suspense movies. Some crank randomly sending threatening letters."

Michelle retrieved the note, deliberately wadded it into a tight ball and chunked it at the wastebasket. "Two points!" She congratulated herself as the ball of paper bounced off the edge and went in.

Then she took another deep, calming breath and picked up the phone.

"Angie, hey. Whatcha doing?"

"Well, it's a lousy TV night so I stopped by the video place and picked up a new release. Want to come join me? It's a thriller. Right up your alley." The sound of her best friend's voice reassured Michelle.

"Thanks, but I think I'll pass. I've had my own thriller here." Michelle was proud to hear that her voice sounded natural.

"Did you have a break-in?"

"No, a threatening letter. It really gave me a start when I opened it, but it was just a prank. One of the guys at the office, I'm sure."

"You're kidding, right?"

"No, serious. It said, 'Someone is watching you.' Of course I just threw it away."

"You should call the police, or at least take it to the post office. It's a federal crime."

"Angela Martin! Do you realize how embarrassing it would be to send up someone I work with for a prank? I'd never work in this town again. I'm sorry I bothered you. Go back to your movie and we'll talk tomorrow."

"If you say so. Give me a call at work. Maybe

we can have lunch."

Michelle tapped her foot impatiently as she glanced at the clock by the restaurant door. Twelve-fifteen. Angela's lateness was customary, but Michelle's one-thirty appointment to show a house added pressure.

Angie burst through the door breathlessly with rushed apologies for being late. When they were seated Angela began the conversation by asking, "Did you change your mind and call the police?"

"No. Nor did I mention it at work. I'm not going to give some creep the satisfaction of even knowing I received it. It's funny though. When I looked around the office this morning and tried to think of each person as that sick type of prankster, not one fit the image."

"Chelle, I think you ought to do something - really!"

Michelle raised an eyebrow. "Maybe so. Something kind of odd did happen this morning. A call came in for me while I was on another line and the man had to wait and wait. Judy asked if he wanted to leave a message or call back but he refused. After all that time he just said, 'Michelle Wilson,' then hung up when I responded."

"That does it. If you won't tell somebody, I will. Accept reality, Chelle. Some nut is stalking you. It happens. It doesn't even have to be someone you know. We live in a dangerous world!"

"Angie, please. A nut may be harassing me and you are becoming hysterical."

"I am *not* hysterical. I don't want to see you get hurt. Do you remember that girl they found in a ditch on the other side of town last year? She was stalked before she disappeared. There have been others, too. Just keep them in mind while you're laughing this off."

"Okay, okay," Michelle agreed. "I'll think about notifying the police."

Everything conspired to make Michelle's afternoon difficult. She barely made it to the house showing, then the man decided he wouldn't do anything until his wife came back from her business trip. When she arrived back at her office at two-fifteen three messages were waiting. The first cancelled a closing she had been working on for weeks; the second required a response before two, and the last simply said that Mr. Someone would be in touch.

Michelle frowned at the last message and buzzed the switchboard operator. "Judy, is this Mr. Someone a joke?"

"I don't know. A man called and left the message when I told him you weren't in."

"Okay, thanks." Michelle hung up the phone and sat staring with a puzzled frown on her face.

In California, Pete Spencer strolled into the trendy restaurant and checked the tables for his friend. He waved to several acquaintances as the maitre d' approached. "Hello, Albert," Pete greeted him. "Has Clint Sharkey come in yet?"

"No, sir, Mr. Spencer, but he did call to reserve a table. Would you prefer to wait for him in the bar or be seated? Your table is ready."

"The table will be fine, Albert. Thanks."

Pete ordered a scotch for himself and a gin and tonic for Clint and looked at his watch. His friend was usually prompt.

Clint and the drinks arrived simultaneously.

"Sorry to keep you waiting," the director apologized. "I had to make a phone call."

"No problem. I just got here in time to order drinks. Working on a new project?"

"Hell, yes. I love my new project. It's the one we were talking about a couple of weeks ago."

"You didn't mention . . . . No, Clint, you didn't. Please tell me you didn't respond to that letter."

"Why not? It's fun. So far three letters, two phone calls. Can't you just see some prim, middle-aged bitch running scared, looking over her shoulder hunting some stalker who's really a thousand miles away?" Wickedness darted from Clint's eyes.

"Have you really lost it?! If you mailed threats that's a federal crime!"

"She can't track me down. I sent one to Raven to mail while she's working in Phoenix, and one to Paul who's shooting around Seattle. Then I drove down to San Diego last night to drop off the third one.

"I'm not stupid, Pete. The calls were made

from pay phones. In fact, I just finished the second one." Clint leaned back and sipped his gin and tonic. "Don't worry. Anyway, it's all in fun. Nobody's going to get hurt."

Pete shook his head. "This is crazy, Clint. You've been watching too many of your own movies. People are starting to get serious about stalking and the one who's most likely to get hurt is you. Stop now before it's too late."

"Back off, Pete. Don't be such a damned spoilsport."

Ann Snuggs

CHAPTER 2

It was almost dark when Michelle reached home that night. Wednesday was her regular day for aerobics at the Y and she had been determined not to let the events of the day get her down. As usual she felt invigorated after the workout and able to face the possibility of discovering another strange letter in the day's mail.

The good feeling faded as she put her key into the lock and realized that the door was not properly secured. Scenes from a hundred movies raced through her head as Michelle mentally debated her choices. Going to get the manager would be embarrassing, yet nothing irritated her any more than a fictional character blissfully and stupidly entering a place with a tampered lock.

Michelle bit her lip and reached inside to hit the light switch, at the same time cursing herself for her stupidity.

She looked around at an apparently undisturbed room, dropped her purse and mail into the nearest chair and thumbed her pepper spray into ready position. Cautiously she began to go through the apartment, for once glad that it was not large. Michelle checked the closets and cabinets and under the bed. Nothing seemed to be out of place or missing except - where was Sultan?

"Sultan? Here, Sultan. Come on, kitty. Sultan, where are you?" Michelle fought back panic. Up until this time she had honestly believed that some so-called friend was playing a prank. Now she was scared.

Quickly Michelle grabbed her phone and speed-dialed the manager, all thoughts of embarrassment wiped away by fear. Two rings. Three rings. Four rings. Of all times for the Johnsons to be out.

"I will not panic. I will not panic. I will not panic," she said aloud in a firm tone. Realizing that she had left the front door standing open, Michelle went back into the living room. She looked carefully at the lock, noting that it gave no indication of having been forced. Mentally debating whether to call the police or wait to talk to the manager - after all the pest control people or some other service could have been careless - Michelle stepped out and scanned the courtyard. Nothing stirred but a slight breeze.

Double Stalk

"Oh!" she stifled a scream as something brushed against her leg. Her fluffy gray cat sat himself at her feet and meowed questioningly.

"Sultan!" Michelle scolded. "Where have you been? And who let you out?" she wondered.

Picking up the cat she turned and reentered the apartment, shutting the door firmly and slamming home the deadbolt.

Later, after feeding both Sultan and herself, she plopped into a comfortable chair and clicked the remote. Tonight she needed something in the way of mindless entertainment. Surely one of the channels would provide that.

Thirty minutes into a program which barely managed to hold her attention Michelle remembered that she had not sorted the mail. She cringed inwardly, then resolutely retrieved the assortment of envelopes and made a quick assessment of each piece. No unmarked envelopes today. "Thank goodness," she breathed with a sigh of relief. The door incident was enough for one day.

During a slack moment at work the next morning Michelle dialed her apartment manager.

"Mr. Johnson, this is Michelle Wilson. Were any servicemen working around my apartment yesterday?"

"Let me think. No, I don't believe . . . . Wait, the handyman came. Had you left any requests?"

"Well, the light over my sink has been blinking but I'm not sure I told you about it."

"I'll check the work list. Why did you want to know?"

"My door was ajar when I got home last night and I know I locked it when I left in the morning. Someone let Sultan out and all-in-all it was disturbing."

"I'll check up on it," Mr. Johnson promised her, "and also make sure that after this servicemen always close doors securely. Don't ever go in if such a thing should happen again, Michelle. That's a dangerous thing to do."

"Like I don't know it," Michelle muttered under her breath as she hung up the phone.

Later that night, after discovering no unnerving letter and having had no questionable phone calls, Michelle felt ready to do something. The next night her off-and-on boyfriend Scott had invited her out for an evening on the town, but she wanted to go out now.

Impulsively she grabbed the phone. "Angie. What are you doing? Let's go to the show."

"I'm loading the dishwasher and was planning to wash my hair. What do you want to see?"

"Wash your hair?! I can't believe I just heard that tired old cliche! You need to get out."

"Actually I was planning to do more than just wash it. I bought one of those new conditioning temporary rinses today and tomorrow your best friend will be a redhead."

"Angie!" Michelle exclaimed, stunned.

Double Stalk

"So you pick up a video at the rental place and come over here," Angie continued. "Anything you want to watch. It will be nice to have someone make sure that the back of my hair is properly saturated. I'll see you in about thirty minutes." Angie broke the connection before Michelle could say another word.

Twenty-five minutes later Michelle, hands full of snacks and her chosen tape, used her elbow to ring Angie's doorbell.

"I can't believe you're going to dye your hair," she said as she placed the video by the TV.

"It's not permanent, just temporary," Angie assured her. "What movie did you get?"

"One of Clint Sharkey's first films."

"Great! Just the thing to go with a quiet evening at home. I don't know why you like any film he's ever done. Every single one of them is so brutal."

"But they're so different."

"That's an understatement!"

"If he would only enlarge his vocabulary. Sometimes I think he knows one word and has someone else write the rest of the dialogue. Then he orchestrates the action. I have to admit he intrigues me."

"Whatever." Angie shrugged. "However, that reminds me. I bought a new *Hollywood Lives* this week and your letter to the editor saying about what you just now said was printed."

"Honest!" Michelle cried. "Let me see it."

"Help me with my hair first. Then you can

read the magazine and we'll watch your movie."

Later Michelle stretched, then contentedly curled up into a ball in the middle of her bed. It had been so nice to experience a day with only normal problems. She was drifting into sleep when the phone shrilled, sending a shock through her body. Her abrupt rising pushed Sultan to the floor and he yowled in protest. With her heart pounding Michelle picked up the receiver.

"Hello."

"Michelle?"

"Yes." Her voice quivered as she tried desperately to decide whether or not the voice was the same as the one she had heard at the office.

The question was answered with his next words. "This is Mr. Someone. I wanted to wish you sweet dreams." A maniacal laugh was cut off by the click of the phone.

Michelle sat shivering, with tears running down her cheeks. Sultan jumped back onto the bed and Michelle gathered him into her arms. "Meow!" he protested and twitched his ears as a tear dropped on him.

Clint hung up the phone still laughing, though in a less theatrical manner. As he started to drive off he noticed that someone was using the pay phone he had left and the uneasy thought crossed his mind that the stranger might have heard what he said.

Double Stalk

By the time he reached Raven's luxurious beach house he had forgotten the man at the phone but still felt set-up over his own call. Clint believed that his innocent-sounding words carried enough menace without being openly threatening.

"You're late, Clint," Raven purred accusingly. "Am I losing my appeal? You used to be early."

Clint kissed her full on the mouth. "No way, Beautiful. I'm working on a project that hung me up. How was Phoenix?"

"Hot and dry. But my part was hot and juicy. Honestly, Clint. This time the critics will love me.

"What was that letter you asked me to mail?" she continued with obvious curiosity. "I did it, but you left off your return address. I started to put it on there . . . ." Raven broke off as a look of consternation swept Clint's face. "What's wrong?"

"You didn't write anything on the envelope, did you?" he asked, his voice husky with sudden panic as all of Pete's warnings flashed through his mind.

"No. Why?" Raven's lovely forehead wrinkled in puzzlement.

Clint paused, then decided to take Raven into his confidence. "That letter was part of my project. I'm playing a prank on a critic and fighting back."

"How can you fight back without identifying yourself?"

"Let's sit down, Raven. It's a long story. Could I have a drink? I need it after that scare you gave me."

Thirty minutes later Raven tossed back her

black hair and stared at Clint, shaking her head in disgust.

"You're mean, Clint," she said levelly. "You've always been careless of people's feelings, but this trick is vicious. Don't you have any grasp of the way stalking can destroy a person's life?"

"Oh, come on, Raven. Shit. No one's life is going to be destroyed by a few letters and phone calls. No one is even coming close to her. You're overreacting."

"No, I'm not. She does not know her stalker is a thousand miles away. Every time a stranger walks by and looks at her or someone dials a wrong number she thinks it's you. If you don't stop this I'm going to tell her. So there." Raven rose and crossed to the bar.

"Okay, okay," Clint conceded. "I'll back off.... Like hell," he finished under his breath.

"Good." Raven handed him a fresh drink and slid down onto the sofa next to him. "Now let's start on another project," she murmured winding her arms around his neck and kissing him deeply.

The following morning back in his own apartment, Clint lit a cigarette and pondered his next move. He wondered if Paul had also noticed the lack of a return address and if he had done anything about it. Clint decided it would be a good idea to check. Flipping through his rolodex he picked up the phone.

It was necessary to work through channels,

but at this point Clint's name had a certain amount of magic in the business and in a few minutes he heard Paul's irritated voice say, "Hello, Clint. What in the hell is so important right now?"

Clint shifted into what Pete called his snake-oil-salesman tone. "Sorry, Paul. I needed to check on that letter I sent you to mail. It was research for a new project, one I might could use you on, and I wanted to make sure you sent it as is."

After Raven's reaction Clint had no intention of telling anyone else the truth.

"Of course I took care of it." Now irritation became anger. "I just read the cover letter and dropped it in the nearest post box as you asked. Damn, Clint, don't you trust me to do things right? It takes a real son-of-a-bitch to stop work for this kind of crap." And with that Paul slammed the phone down.

Clint hung up and tapped his ear, which was ringing from the sharp disconnection. "I'll show you a real son-of-a-bitch," he said to the dead receiver, his quicksilver temper flaring. "You won't work on my next film, good part for you or not."

He picked up the morning paper and began to look for the appropriate letters to spell his next message. When the doorbell rang he was half through. Scissors dangling from his hand, Clint started to rise, then sank back watching the door open as Pete let himself into the apartment.

"You look guilty to me," his friend greeted him.

"Don't screw around with me today," Clint

snarled. "I'm already pissed off."

Pete dropped easily into the nearest chair. His tolerance of the director's moods was the chief reason they had managed to maintain a good working relationship for several years.

"What are you doing here?" Clint demanded.

Pete smiled disarmingly. "You're my friend, remember? I was in the neighborhood and thought I'd drop by."

"That's crap. I'd see you tonight at Joey's party and you never 'drop by' at this hour. If you're out this early there's a purpose. Now cut the shit and tell me why you're here." Clint scowled at his friend resentfully.

"Who broke your toy, Clint? You aren't usually this hostile any more than I usually get up this early."

"Okay, you win. I called Paul and we had words. It warped my world view. How's that for someone who, according to Miss-Bitch-in-Hicksville, has no vocabulary?"

Pete laughed but quickly sobered. "That's why I'm here. Raven called me right after you left this morning. Why in the hell did you tell her what you've been doing? She was serious about blowing the whistle on you if you don't stop. Then when I come over to warn you I find you with incriminating evidence in hand. I'm the one who ought to be pissed, Clint. I told you from the very first this long-distance stalking was a bad idea." He broke off and ran a hand through his hair nervously.

"Do you realize how much trouble you're in if

Raven talks? In this town all she has to do is drop a hint. You've made a lot of enemies on the way up. Just one of those coupled with the current media climate could ruin you. Gentlemen's agreements went the way of the dinosaur. No reporter will look the other way when he can make a buck."

"Maybe you're right, Pete," Clint admitted grudgingly. "Still, I hate to give it up. You can't imagine how much I've enjoyed concocting this plot."

"Well write it instead of doing it. Live it vicariously. I'm not saying this as a spoilsport. If you keep it up you may find yourself in real trouble. I don't want to see that happen." He grinned. "Can you see me in a film written and directed by Prisoner Number 587306648?"

"If so the charge would be murder rather than stalking because anybody who turns me in would die."

"Great! Now we add terroristic threatening. Clint, go back to writing. Put this plot on paper. Start a new screenplay. Anything besides continuing your harassment of some stranger. Sooner or later you'll get caught."

After Pete left Clint sat and brooded. He knew that his friend was telling the truth and he was playing a dangerous game, but he loved living on the edge. Abruptly Clint snatched the papers from the table, wadded them up and tossed them into the wastebasket. Okay, he would give up the mailings.

His stalking technique would be telephone only. Enough pay phones existed in the metro area to use a different one each time and call for weeks. Another plus would be that he could honestly tell Raven there would be no more letters. Not that he minded lying to her, he had done it many times in the past, but it gave him a type of perverse pleasure to know he would not be lying about the letters.

CHAPTER 3

Michelle was straightening papers on her desk in preparation for leaving when her phone rang.

"Yes?"

"Michelle, this is Mr. Johnson. Mr. Zachary came this morning with the parts to fix your light. He was in your apartment yesterday but he's sure he closed the door securely. However, he did see a man loitering around the apartment next to yours. A blond man, he said. Do you know anyone like that?"

"Mr. Johnson, I know any number of blond men. Did Mr. Zachary notice anything else about him?"

"Well, he didn't mention it. I can ask him."

"Please do. I'm on my way to the police

station now. I received a disturbing phone call last night and it wasn't the first one. It's time for me to get some help. I really need to go so I'll talk to you later."

"Sit down, Miss Wilson," Detective Lucisi said. "You sounded upset when you called. What can we do for you?"

"I feel embarrassed about calling the police for what must be a prank, but I've been getting strange phone calls and have received one threatening letter. It's unnerved me and, quite honestly, I'm not the nervous type." Her voice began to tremble and she finished hurriedly, "I didn't know where else to turn."

Lucisi studied her silently for a moment with his piercing black eyes then smiled encouragingly. "You came to the right place. When did these calls start?"

"It seems like ages ago but actually they began this week."

"Do they follow a particular pattern? Any special time of day? Maybe a set interval of time between calls?"

Michelle paused to think and Lucisi could almost see the wheels turning in her mind.

"Take your time," he said, using the quiet interval to fully appreciate the attractive view she presented.

Slowly Michelle shook her head and her blue eyes looked directly into his black ones. "I don't see a pattern. He called me at work twice. Then last night, a little after midnight. He uses the name 'Mr. Someone'."

"'Mr. Someone?' That sounds pretty theatrical."

"Once he called the office while I was out and left a message from Mr. Someone. Then last night he introduced himself as Mr. Someone when he called to wish me sweet dreams." Michelle shuddered. "As if I slept enough to have any dreams after that."

"Okay. Do you have the letter with you?"

"No, I threw it away."

"Threw it away! That wasn't very bright. I'm sorry." he added quickly seeing the look of embarrassment on her face. "I didn't mean to be rude, but why would you throw it away?"

"I told you I thought it was a prank. At first I thought it was someone at work or some friend. My friends kid me about my taste in movies - I watch a lot of thrillers - and it just didn't strike me as serious."

"Sending threats through the mail is always serious. It's a federal crime. Can you remember what the letter said?"

"I can describe it exactly. The letters were cut from a newspaper, not all caps but from headlines. They were pasted on approximately one-half of a piece of typing paper torn across the top, I didn't notice whether or not it was bond, and it said, 'Someone is watching you.'"

"Nice concise description."

Michelle smiled slightly. "Thank you."

"What about the envelope? Where was it cancelled? Were there markings of any kind on it?"

"I can't remember." Michelle looked at him blankly. "Detective Lucisi, I don't know what happened to the envelope."

"Great! We'll start there. You're sure you didn't throw it away, too?"

Michelle nodded.

"Then do this for me. Go home and look for the envelope. It has to be postmarked. If it isn't, somebody with access to your mailbox is your stalker. As far as the phone calls are concerned the Caller ID service offered by the phone company is the easiest tracer available. Order that today. Of course some phones block the ID process but we could be lucky. Bring me the envelope when you find it."

"All right, I will, but there's something else you ought to know."

Lucisi had risen as Michelle stood to go. Now he sat back down and gestured for her to do the same. "I prefer to hear everything here." Once again he gave her his gentle smile. "It's easier for me to make notes. I spend too much time standing around juggling my notebook. So when I don't have to, I don't."

"Night before last when I got home my door was ajar."

"And you went in?" he interrupted, obviously shocked. "Surely if you watch thrillers you know how dangerous that is. For a change movies do not distort reality in that incidence."

"I know. I know," Michelle admitted shamefacedly. "If I hadn't already known I certainly would now. Everyone has fussed at me about it. But it was embarrassing to think of calling anyone."

"That attitude is the one *most* helpful to criminals," the detective lectured her sternly. "People seem to prefer being robbed or attacked to appearing foolish and that viewpoint is the most foolish of all."

"Okay. Now shall I finish?"

Lucisi nodded.

"I was lucky. No one was waiting in the apartment and the handyman had been in there while I was at work. He says he closed the door but he could be mistaken. However, just as I was leaving the office to come down here my apartment manager called and told me that Mr. Zachary, he's the handyman, said someone had been loitering around my building. Mr. Johnson, the manager, asked if I knew any blond men but such a vague description could fit a lot of people, including the policeman sitting at the desk behind me."

"Was anything missing from your apartment?"

"No, not that I've noticed, nor was anything disturbed. That's another reason I waited to report this."

"All right. Give me your manager's phone number and yours - work, cell and home. I'll try to talk with both the manager and the maintenance man today. Be sure to call me when you find the envelope."

Michelle glanced at her watch as she left the police station, just enough time to check her calls at the office and contact the buyer who had stalled her earlier before taking an early lunch. Maybe it would be a good idea to grab a sandwich at her apartment and look for the envelope. Not only was her curiosity aroused but she wouldn't mind spending a little more time with Detective Lucisi. He was certainly easy on the eyes.

After Michelle left the police station the blond detective at the desk by Lucisi's commented, "You certainly jumped right in on that report, Tommy. Mail threats are not exactly in your department."

"Hey, man. I'll work this one on my own time. Anonymous threateners interest me."

"Uh-huh. Right. I saw what interested you when she walked in the door."

"Okay. Any way you look at it there's a bonus for me in this case." He picked up the phone and dialed the apartment manager's number.

When she reached her apartment Michelle noted gratefully that her door was securely locked. She dropped her purse into a chair and knelt by the coffee table. After all, the letter itself had almost escaped her notice when Sultan had scattered the mail. She looked carefully under the table and the sofa and chairs by it. No envelope. Sultan joined her, his nose next to hers. Michelle stroked his soft fur.

"Where could it be, Sultan?" she puzzled as she sat back on her heels. Then it dawned on her. "I'll bet you do know. You've been playing with it, haven't you?"

Michelle was half-way under the bed reaching for what she hoped was the envelope when the doorbell rang. "Terrific," she muttered. "Who could that be?" Catching the paper between her first two fingers she crawled out backwards and went to answer the bell.

Detective Lucisi was ringing for the second time when Michelle opened the door. "Oh, it's you!" she exclaimed brushing back her hair.

He smiled. "I hope I'm not interrupting, but I was talking to the manager and he said he had seen you come in. Did you find the envelope?"

"I think so." The detective raised a questioning eyebrow as Michelle looked at the paper in her hand. "I was pulling this from under the bed when you rang. Yes, this is it, just as it came with the exception of Sultan's additions. See," she held it out to him, "tooth and claw marks. Sultan loves to play with papers."

Dectective Lucisi took the envelope. He studied it carefully and frowned. "Do you know anyone who's been on vacation lately? Look at the postmark. Phoenix."

Michelle thought for a moment then shook her head slowly. "Not a soul. Detective Lucisi, how could someone in Phoenix even know my address? Why would anybody there want to threaten me here?"

"Call me Tom. I don't have the faintest idea. This gets more like *Alice in Wonderland*, curiouser and curiouser. Did you call the phone company? If the calls are also coming from Phoenix we'll need to call in federal authorities right away."

"Not yet. I will as soon as I get back to the office." She looked at her watch. "My lunch hour is practically gone."

As Michelle was locking her door she noticed the mail truck pulling out of the parking lot. "Wait," she said. "Let me check my mail while you're here. I'll work late tonight to make up for lunch." They went back inside.

When Michelle returned with a handful of items she dropped the catalogs and magazines and handed the envelopes to Lucisi. He quickly sorted them, pulling one from the stack. "This looks similar but has a Seattle postmark. Here, open it."

Michelle regarded it with the same repulsion she would have given a snake. "You open it. At this point I don't even want to touch it."

Lucisi gave her his enchanting smile. "Lady, don't you know it's a crime to open someone else's mail?"

Returning the smile she took the missive gingerly. "Okay. If my heart stops from sheer terror it's your fault." She opened the envelope and pulled out another half page like the first one, handing it to the detective without even looking at it.

"This one says, 'Someone will be seeing you.' I'd say it's from the same person and that person has returned from a trip West. Are you sure someone you know, not necessarily a friend, maybe a casual acquaintance, hasn't been on vacation recently?"

"Not to my knowledge. But I will check around. Now I really need to get back to work."

"How about we discuss this over dinner?" suggested Lucisi as they walked to their respective cars.

"Thank you, but I'm afraid I already have plans for tonight."

"Here's my number." He pulled a card from his pocket and scribbled on the back then offered it to Michelle. "If he calls again contact me immediately."

"But today's Friday. Do you work tomorrow?"

"My home and cell numbers are there on the back. Until we get a better reading on this guy we can't know whether or not he's dangerous. If you hear anything I want to know."

Michelle tucked the card into her purse. "You've been awfully nice. Thank you for not treating me like an hysterical fool."

"No problem. You are neither. Call me if he calls you," the detective reiterated as he got into his car.

As she had promised, Michelle ordered Caller ID when she returned to the office. She also called Scott and asked him to pick her up one-half hour later than the original plan.

"I'll tell you all about it over dinner," she assured him when he asked why.

All-in-all Michelle felt satisfied with her day as she put the finishing touches on her make-up before

Scott arrived. It had never been easy for her to ask for help, yet her experience with the police had been a breeze. Due to that good-looking Detective Lucisi, she admitted to herself. He seemed to find her attractive and, goodness knows, he was certainly a treat to her eyes. She'd have to be careful what she said to Scott about him. Thank heavens she and Scott didn't have any commitments. Why just last week when she and Angie went to the show they had seen him with a date. No strings. With luck Detective Lucisi - Tom, she corrected herself - would ask her to dinner again.

The jangle of the phone interrupted her musings and her heart jerked as if the ring had been a shot. Michelle cursed herself mentally for not taking the time to buy a Caller ID display box on the way home. She picked up the receiver uneasily.

"Hello."

"Chelle, you don't sound like yourself. Are you all right? What's wrong?"

"Angie, it's you." Michelle practically melted with relief. "I have a long story to tell you but Scott will be here any minute. Let me give you a call first thing in the morning. Can you go shopping with me?"

"Sure thing. I'll see you then."

Clint, drink in hand, scanned the patio full of people. He loved to work a crowd and parties at Joey Miller's were always good places to do business. A well-endowed blonde starlet fluttered her fingers at him from the far side of the patio. Clint smiled and acknowledged the wave by lifting his drink but made no move to join her. His eyes flicked across the mass of bodies searching for a particular producer he felt sure would be present. He turned quickly as a heavy hand clapped him on the shoulder.

"Hey, Joey," Clint greeted his host. "Terrific party."

"Yeah. Mine always are," Miller said smugly. "The best of everything. I see Mandy Meyer trying to get your attention."

"The bitch wants me to write something especially for her. I don't know why. You could hardly call my films women's pictures."

Joey smiled slyly. "Maybe what she really wants is the writer, not the script."

"Another big-name notch on her gun? Could be. Changing the subject, have you seen Ethan Hosler? He told me he would be here tonight."

"Not yet, but he's coming. The stuff's too good for him to miss my party. There's Mark Whitfield. I need to talk to him. See you later."

Clint drifted back toward the bar. A soft hand on his arm slowed him and he looked down into Raven's big dark eyes.

"Hi, Raven. I'm on my way for a refill. What can I get for you?"

"White wine will be fine."

Clint and Raven slowly snaked through the crowd, greeting acquaintances as they worked their way to the far side of the pool where they found two empty chairs.

"You know I'm really pissed at you for calling Pete." Clint's voice was calm but venom shot from his eyes. "You have no frigging right to butt into my affairs."

Raven regarded him coolly. "TS, Sweetie. I told you how I felt about your cute little harassment game and what I will do if you don't stop."

"Right. And I told you that I would back off. I want to know why the hell you had to go and drag Pete into it." He grabbed her forearm. "Let's hear your damn explanation."

"Take your hand off of me, Clint. Right now. You can figure it out for yourself, you piece of shit." Raven jerked her arm from his grasp and stalked away.

"Lover's quarrel?" asked a voice from behind Clint.

"Ethan. Good to see you." Clint held out his hand. "Sit down. I have a new story going that just might interest you."

CHAPTER 4

The blond man watched from his nook in the hedge as Scott opened the car door for Michelle. In his mind's eye he was the one escorting the woman he adored. Tonight's date was no threat to the hidden man's yearnings. In his careful inventory of the people who surrounded Michelle, the man with her now definitely belonged in the 'friend' category. The observer had seen him many times and was comfortable about his presence.

When they left the apartment complex the blond man tailed the car. He determined their destination and made his way to his own living quarters.

A hostess seated the couple in a corner booth.

"Good," Michelle commented. "This is nice and private. You are not going to believe the story I have to tell."

"Have the names been changed to protect the innocent?" Scott asked whimsically.

"No, you may hear the true story. I never thought anything like this could ever happen to me. It started Monday. Or was it Tuesday? I've lost track."

"Super-efficient Wilson loses track of days?" exclaimed Scott. "I can hardly wait to hear the tale." He broke off as the waiter offered menus. Being familiar with the restaurant's bill of fare they quickly ordered and Michelle began to speak again.

Scott listened in amazed silence then pushed back his empty plate, leaned against the cushioned seat and shook his head. "I can't believe it. You don't make enemies, Chelle. People like you."

"Stalkers don't necessarily dislike their targets. Sometimes they are fascinated by them. That sounds kind of conceited, doesn't it?"

"Not at all. I understand what you're saying."

"The detective asked if I knew anyone who had been on vacation. I can't think of a soul. Can you?"

Scott thought for a moment. "Only person I can think of is Shawn Karlyn, one of the guys at my office."

"Do I know him? The name doesn't ring a bell."

"He's about my height, blond, average build. Maybe you met him at the Fourth of July gala we attended. I can't remember."

"Is he home yet?"

"He's due back Monday. We don't talk enough for me to be aware of his exact plans."

"The man Mr. Zachary saw at the apartments was blond. Does the agency have some type of brochure with Shawn Karlyn's picture in it? I'd like for Mr. Zachary to see him without bringing the police into the matter. It would be less embarrassing for all of us to handle it unobtrusively. If Mr. Karlyn wasn't even in town that day he couldn't be the one."

"I should be able to locate one somewhere. Our pictures appear in the newspaper ads sometimes. I'll check Monday."

Disappointment clouded Michelle's eyes. She had hoped Scott would offer to go to his office tomorrow, but she smiled and said, "Thanks. Please let me know as soon as you find a picture. This matter is getting on my nerves."

Clint left the party in a foul mood. His flare-up with Raven coupled with the coolness Ethan showed toward his new idea put a bad taste in his mouth that could not be altered in spite of the variety of chemicals he had poured into his system. He drove too fast and quickly arrived at his apartment in time to realize that he was not ready to call it a night. Spinning the wheel, Clint left rubber on the parking lot and sped down the street. He found himself headed south along the coast. After thirty minutes or so of fast driving he began to mellow and finally stopped at a little bar.

Only a few customers remained in the dimly-lighted room. Clint slid onto a barstool and looked around.

"What'll it be?" A muscular bartender so stereotypical that Clint felt he had been sent from Central Casting stood in front of him.

"I'll have a . . ." Clint caught himself before saying his usual gin and tonic. "I'll have a Miller Lite."

The bartender set a can and a glass in front of Sharkey. "Two-fifty."

Clint fished out exact change and shoved it across the bar. "Is there a pay phone in here?"

The big man pointed to a booth in back without comment.

Beer in hand Clint moved to the phone. He stepped into the booth and pulled the door closed, marveling at the old-fashioned cabinet-like structure. He dropped in some coins and dialed the now-familiar number.

"Hello."

"Hi, Michelle. How are you?" Clint made his tone soft and caressing.

Click. The phone went dead in Clint's hand.

"Bitch!" He swore under his breath and redialed. After ten rings with no answer he replaced the receiver then immediately redialed. He could make that phone ring forever if she wouldn't cooperate with him. For almost half an hour he dialed and redialed, keeping the ringing persistent.

The steady ringing seemed to grow louder in her ears and finally Michelle could stand it no longer. She picked up the phone reluctantly and held it to her ear but said nothing.

In California, Clint was sitting in the phone booth, eyes on his watch. He had determined to call and re-call thirty minutes before leaving and driving home. If the bar didn't have closing time he would consider ringing all night and be glad to do it. But he wanted to be gone before then in hopes that no one in this place would remember him.

Then he heard the sound of Michelle lifting the phone and almost held his breath in anticipation of her choice of greeting. Certainly he, Clint Sharkey, would be spouting expletives at anyone who initiated such an attack on him.

No sound came across the wire. Clint thought that Michelle had simply answered and put the receiver aside until he heard the faint sound of her breathing.

"Michelle, I know you're there. Say something to me."

Quiet remained on the other end of the line. Clint's temper flared. All of the rejection he had experienced throughout the evening added viciousness to his words.

"Listen, bitch, if you ever hang up on me again I *will* come after you. Don't think I won't and don't you forget it." He slammed the receiver down violently, shaking with anger. A tap on the booth made him jerk around to discover the bartender staring at him through the glass. Clint opened the door.

"Look, Buddy, I'm closing up here. You'll have to find an outside phone some place to fight with your girlfriend."

The shock of the big man having heard at least part of his call drained the rage from the director. "Okay," he said meekly.

Michelle tried to remain calm but realized that she was trembling from the fury of Clint's outburst. His words echoed over and over again in her mind.

Suddenly it dawned on her that his threat implied a previous non-threat. Quickly she turned on the light and began to search for pencil and paper. Michelle repeated Clint's statements aloud until she managed to write word-for-word what she had heard on the phone. She remembered the emphasis on "will" when he said, "I *will* come after you." Surely that meant whoever the threatener was had no intention of actually bothering her now.

Comforting herself with that thought Michelle went back to bed. Sleep had almost overcome her when she remembered Detective Lucisi insisting that he be contacted if the stalker called again. The clock on the bed table read two forty-five. Doubtless he had not meant for her to disturb his sleep. She settled under the covers mentally promising herself to call him early the next morning, before she left to go shopping with Angie.

Michelle woke to bright sunshine and Sultan nuzzling her ear. Eight thirty-five. She had overslept. In spite of the night's disruptions she felt alert and ready to face the day.

While she was still dressing the phone rang. Her heart jumped then she resolutely answered.

"Miss Wilson?"

"Yes." The voice was familiar, not that of the stalker, but she couldn't place it immediately.

"This is Tom Lucisi. The detective you spoke with yesterday," he added when Michelle did not respond at once.

"Of course. I remember you. I'm a bit rushed and it was a full night."

"You heard from your caller?"

"Yes, around two this morning."

"Why didn't you call me?"

"At two a.m.? Certainly you don't think I would wake you up to tell you about something that you could hear just as easily now. I was planning to phone you before I left home. And I *am* buying a display box or a Caller ID phone today."

"Did the man identify himself as 'Mr. Someone'?"

"No. When I heard his voice I hung up on him. He called back and back and back for what felt like forever. I wanted to ignore it but finally couldn't stand it any longer so I answered. He was furious.

He cursed at me and slammed the receiver hard. I wrote down exactly what he said. Would you like to hear it?"

"Very much."

"Hold on. Let me get the notepad."

Michelle read the message and added, "The way he snarled, 'I *will* come after you,' made me think that this is some kind of game for him, that there's no real intention to harm me."

"Don't ever think that way. It gives the perpetrator the edge. If you get careless it can open doors for him.

"What are your plans for today? Will you have someone with you?"

Michelle started to bristle at his inquisitiveness until she recognized that he was concerned about her safety.

"This morning a friend and I are going shopping and will probably have lunch somewhere. We didn't make a schedule," she finished dryly.

"Perhaps I could meet you for lunch."

"Well," Michelle hesitated, "I'm not sure exactly where we're going or what time we'll get there. I don't mean to put you off but we planned to play the day by ear. We didn't schedule any specific place at any specific time."

"That being the case, why not phone me when you get home? I'll help you hook up your Caller ID."

"Fine. It may be into the afternoon though."

"No problem. I plan to watch some football on TV so I'll be home whenever you call."

Michelle had hardly hung up when the phone rang again.

"Chelle, what time are you picking me up?"

"Could we go in your car, Angie?"

"Sure. Having car trouble on top of everything else?"

"No, but I want you to come home with me when we finish shopping. I'll tell you why when I see you. What time?"

"About thirty minutes okay?"

"Make it closer to forty-five."

"Fine. See you then."

When they were settled in Angie's car she turned to Michelle and asked, "Where do you want to go first?"

"I guess the Central Mall. It has almost every kind of store."

"Now catch me up on what's been happening," Angie demanded as she pulled out of the parking lot.

"You will be overjoyed to learn that I did what you wanted me to do. Yesterday morning I went to the police."

"Good! It's about time."

"Well, I've had two scary late-night phone calls and the handyman, Mr. Zachary, said that he had seen a man around the apartments, so I decided it had reached that point. I was really afraid, Angie. After the first call in the night I went to pieces. I was ashamed of myself later, but . . ."

"Chelle! You were out of control? You're always so cool about everything!"

"Yeah, that in itself pretty much clued me in that it was time to go for help. I don't fall apart like that."

"So how did it go with the cops?"

"Terrific! By the luck of the draw the detective who is handling my case is tall, dark and handsome. Seriously. Well, actually, he's not tall tall, but tall enough. He's also very concerned and considerate - he called this morning to check on me - and is coming over this afternoon to hook up the Caller ID we will be buying this morning. That's why I wanted you to drive, so you can meet him and tell me what you think. Wait till you see his smile."

"What's this dream detective's name?"

"Tom. Tom Lucisi. Have you ever met him?"

"Not me. My life doesn't often cross the path of policemen. Unless they're traffic cops."

Michelle laughed. "Meeting Tom - he's already told me to call him 'Tom' - should be a much more pleasant experience than your traffic cop encounters."

After making stops at several stores both women were loaded with packages.

"Shall we go somewhere else for lunch or stop at one of the restaurants here at the mall?" Angie asked as she dropped onto a handy bench to redistribute her purchases.

"Whatever you like. I wouldn't mind eating at Martinelli's. They have wonderful lasagne. Actually everything there is delicious. Are you in the mood for Italian?"

"Sounds great to me. What I like best is their made-from-scratch pizza. No standard pizza place ever made it so good. Do you want to put this stuff in the car first?"

"Okay. That's probably the best thing to do. Then we won't have to keep an eye on it while we're eating."

Neither woman noticed when a blond man left the mall a short distance behind them nor when he strolled leisurely into the restaurant after they had been seated.

Michelle was half-finished with her spaghetti with house sauce and meatballs when Angie said, "The next time you can do it without being obvious glance at the man in the fourth booth against the front wall. He seems to be staring at us."

"What does he look like?"

"Kind of heavyset - not fat - but solid. Sandy-blond hair. Nothing I can see to make him especially noticeable except that he keeps looking this way."

Michelle continued eating for a few minutes before looking around as if hunting a waitress. She flagged one down and asked for more tea then told Angie, "I don't remember ever seeing him before, do you?"

"He's not familiar to me, but he's so ordinary-looking; he wouldn't stand out in a crowd."

"The man Mr. Zachary saw at the apartments was blond. Are you finished? Just knowing a strange man is watching us makes me nervous."

Angie threw a quick glance at her friend,

surprised to observe the extent of her edginess. "Sure. I'll take the rest of my pizza with me. If we don't eat it your pizza-eating cat will."

"Okay. Let's go."

After they had paid and were leaving the restaurant Michelle noticed that the man was gone. She nudged Angie and indicated the empty booth. "Guess we didn't have to hurry after all."

"That's okay. We'll head on back to your place and call your gorgeous friend, Detective Adonis."

"Oh, Angie. His name is Detective Lucisi and he's not mine."

"Yet! They all fall for you sooner or later. The man in Martinelli's probably just liked your looks," she added as they reached the car.

CHAPTER 5

But it was another hour before they reached Michelle's apartment, for each thought of several stops that needed to be made, including the grocery store.

Michelle and Angie hoisted the loaded sacks onto the kitchen counter with relief.

"Why are my groceries always so heavy?" complained Michelle. "It's not like I cook gourmet dinners every night."

"Mine are the same. Do you want to unpack the groceries or the car?"

"The car, definitely. It will be nice to let someone else put up the food. Don't forget to leave out all the ingredients for this fancy recipe you promised to make tonight. That was a good idea.

We haven't cooked-in together in a long time."

Michelle stood by the trunk of the car busily sorting her sacks from Angie's and never noticed the faded maroon Ford at the back of the parking lot.

The blond man had been delayed in following Michelle and Angie from the grocery store but he reached the parking lot of the apartments in time to observe Michelle as she returned to Angie's car to retrieve the packages.

He loved to watch her move. His eyes ran up and down her body as she twisted around juggling the sacks, sorting her own bags from those of her friend. He studied every part of her, imprinting her shape in his mind and licking his lips at the thought of touching her form.

The onlooker sighed as Michelle disappeared from his view. He turned the key in the ignition in preparation to leave, but changed his mind at the thought that Michelle and Angie might go out again after storing the purchases.

Michelle carried her packages to the bedroom and deposited them on the bed. Rifling through them she found the Caller ID phone and pulled it from its carton.

"This appears to be super-simple to hook up," Michelle commented to her friend as Angie came into the room. "Maybe we should just do it ourselves."

Double Stalk

"And make me miss out on meeting Detective Wonderful? Not a chance. Get on that phone and invite him over here."

Detective Lucisi observed the man in the maroon Ford parked at the back of the parking lot as a matter of course. He noted that the car's paint was worn in spots and the license plate was covered with dirt. He was considering moving in for a closer look when Michelle opened the door.

"Hi, Detective . . . Tom," she greeted him.

"Miss Wilson," he returned with a slight nod.

"Call me Michelle."

"Michelle."

"Come on in. This is my friend, Angela Martin."

Angie grinned. "Call me Angie."

"Hi, Angie." Tom Lucisi offered his hand.

"When I saw how easily this thing hooked up I was sort of ashamed to bother you."

Lucisi flashed his disarming smile. "I would have been concerned if I hadn't heard from you since you said you'd call.

"Where are you going to put it?"

"On the stand by my bed. In here." Michelle motioned toward the bedroom.

As the detective passed her Angie mouthed to Michelle behind his back, "Very nice!"

Michelle signaled her agreement.

The two friends watched as Lucisi quickly programmed the phone and turned to Michelle.

"It's ready to go. Is there someone you can phone who will call you right back to check it?"

"Sure. I'll call Mr. Johnson. Someone should be home this time of day." She punched in the number and made her request. The three of them watched as the phone rang and the manager's number was displayed. Michelle picked up the receiver.

"Thanks, Mrs. Johnson. I appreciate your help." She looked up at Tom. "And I thank you, too. You were nice to come give us a hand."

"My pleasure," he responded as he moved toward the living room.

Michelle sent a quick, questioning glance to Angie which her friend answered with a concurring motion of her head.

"We're eating in tonight. Angie's whipping up some marvelous casserole recipe and I'll make a green salad. We cheated and stopped by the bakery for dessert. Would you like to join us?"

"If you're sure it's not an imposition, I'd love to."

"Great!

"Angie, how long does this concoction take?"

"You'd better give me a couple of hours. What time do you want to eat?"

Michelle looked at Tom. "Are you hungry? Did you have a big lunch?"

Lucisi laughed. "Only if you call beer and chips a good meal. By the time I thought about eating it was after one and I was afraid if I got out in traffic I might miss your call."

"Then it's all my fault you're hungry. Quick, Angie, get started. It's already four-thirty." Angie vanished into the kitchen.

"Sit down, Tom." Michelle gestured to a chair. "Tell me why you decided to become a detective."

Tom chose a seat on the couch and commented, "That's an interesting conversation starter."

Michelle ducked her head, abashed, then grinned and said, "Sorry. I've always been interested in crime. First it was Nancy Drew and the Hardy Boys, then I moved on to more realistic detective fiction. Did I tell you how much my friends kid me about the movies I watch?"

"I believe you mentioned something along those lines. With that kind of attitude it surprises me you didn't enlist police help sooner."

"It seemed so absurd to think someone might be after me. If a friend had been threatened I'd probably have been the first to insist on official involvement. Who knows?" She shrugged, then her face changed, mirroring a sudden thought. "With all the activity today I haven't checked the mail. I'll do it now." Michelle snatched up her keys and started for the door.

"Wait, Michelle. Let me go with you. When I came in I meant to ask you about a car in the parking lot and it slipped my mind. A man was sitting in an old maroon Ford at the back. He may have been picking someone up but I just had the feeling that he was watching the place. I was thinking about checking him out when you opened the door." Tom smiled. "The sight of you drove everything else from my mind."

"Oh, yeah. Right. Detective Lucisi, lines like that went out with love beads and flower children. Although I am flattered."

He chuckled. "Sorry. Sounded all right to me.

"Do you know somebody in these apartments who drives a car like that?" he persisted. "Or have you seen the car itself?"

Michelle shook her head. "It doesn't belong here unless we have a new renter. The clientele here is pretty stable, but I could ask Mr. Johnson."

"I wish you would. Now let's go get the mail."

Calling back to let Angie know where they were going, Michelle and Tom went to the rack of mailboxes and soon returned with the usual handful of mail.

Michelle hurriedly shuffled through the stack. "This looks questionable." She ripped the envelope open and handed the page to Lucisi.

He unfolded it and smiled. "This is a threat to represent you." The detective held out the flyer to Michelle. "Somebody wants your vote."

At that moment Angie came in from the kitchen and plopped into a chair. "Finally. The food is in the oven. One hour till dinner.

"Anything exciting in the mail."

"Not so far," Michelle responded. She continued to sort through the stack in her lap.

"Uh-oh. Here it is. Postmark San Diego. No return address. Unseal it, Tom. Pretend you're my secretary if it bothers you to open another person's letters." She tossed it into his lap.

Tom slit the envelope with his pocket knife and pulled out a half-page with pasted letters forming the message. "You're right. This one says, 'Someone will be in touch.' He must like variety. It's unusual to see different phrasing in these types of cases. More often they all say the same thing."

"Do you specialize in cases of threats?" Angie asked. "It doesn't seem like it would be very common around here."

"Actually I did a little research last night. Here, threats are more likely to involve face-to-face altercations, usually between friends, neighbors and family members."

"Do you think that the variety in the messages is a clue of some sort?" puzzled Michelle.

"Ah, here goes Sherlock Holmes. She's solving the mystery for us," Angie teased.

"It could have some significance," Lucisi admitted. "At the moment I'm not sure just what, but don't quit thinking it out."

"I'll think while I work," said Michelle, rising from her seat. "It's time to start fixing the salad. Do you eat all kinds of salad greenery, Tom?"

"I eat most everything," he replied with a smile.

After Michelle went into the kitchen, Angie turned to the detective. "Could I see the threat? The first one Chelle threw away and the second you took. I'd like to see one." She studied it carefully then handed it back to Lucisi. "Do you think she's in any real danger?"

Tom shrugged. "Who knows? It's hard to know exactly how to tell. With postmarks as far apart as Phoenix, Seattle and San Diego, and all of those being so far away from here . . . ." His words trailed off.

"Changing the subject, or at least switching to another aspect, do you know anyone who drives a faded maroon Ford?"

Angie paused to think then shook her head. "No. Why?"

"One was parked at the back of the parking lot when I arrived. Someone was just sitting there, apparently not coming or going. Michelle said she didn't think it belonged to anyone living in these apartments."

"Has she told you about the man watching us at lunch?"

"No. Suppose you tell me."

"We were eating at Martinelli's at the mall . . ."

"With my aunt," he interjected.

"I'm sorry? No one was there except the two of us."

Lucisi grinned. "Martinelli's belongs to my aunt. Go ahead. I shouldn't have interrupted you."

"There's not much to tell. A blond man was sitting in the booth on the front wall watching us. Chelle got really nervous and insisted that we leave but we noticed he was gone when we left the restaurant."

"Had either of you seen him earlier in the day? Was he in any other places where you shopped?"

"Couldn't prove it by me. He was so average-looking. If I hadn't glanced up just in time to catch his stare I would have paid no attention to him at lunch. Blond is the only description I can give you and, in all honesty, I'm not sure I would know him again if I saw him."

"Then let's hope he's not our man. I want this guy to stand out in a crowd."

Michelle stuck her head around the corner. "Angie, would you set the table?" She nodded toward it. "Of course, you'll have to clear it first."

Tom followed Angie into the kitchen. "Tell me about the man in Martinelli's. He slacked his body against the counter.

"There's not much to tell."

Lucisi laughed out loud.

"And what was so funny about that?" Michelle demanded.

"You and Angie sound just alike. Those were her exact words."

Michelle smiled. "Yeah, people tell us we can communicate without words because we think the same way.

"She had a better view of him than I did. We were at one of the tables, kind of in the middle, and he was sitting at a booth by the wall. You know how Martinelli's is set up?"

"Yes, he does," answered Angie as she came in to get the plates. "It's his aunt's restaurant."

"Really? Now I'm sorry I asked you to dinner. Everything there is so good and . . ."

"Thanks a bunch, Chelle," Angie broke in. "Are you implying that I can't cook?"
"Of course not, Angie."

CHAPTER 6

Clint opened his eyes and immediately shut them, wincing at the light streaming through the window. What a monster hangover! Surely he hadn't had that much last night. Then he remembered his wild drive and the phone call. Maybe the beer at the bar on the highway had been the step over the line. Clint vaguely recalled some saying from high school. The exact wording eluded him, but the essence was not to drink beer on top of whiskey. Whoever said it must have been right.

Keeping his eyes closed, he slowly attempted to sit up. Waves of nausea joined his headache. Clint sank back, then determinedly rolled over and pushed himself to a sitting position on the side of the bed. Breathing deeply, he held on to the mattress and tried to pull himself together, physically and mentally.

"I will not throw up. I will not throw up," he told himself stubbornly. His will power was not up to the task and he ran for the bathroom.

An hour or so later Clint was propped in a large chair with an ice pack on his head and a Bloody Mary in his hand. The shrill of the doorbell jarred his entire body and he snarled:

"Who in hell wants in at dawn on Saturday morning!"

The sound of the lock unfastening announced Pete, the only other person who currently had a key.

"It's afternoon," Pete remarked casually. He stared at his friend, grinned and shook his head. "You look like hell."

"I've frigging been there. What in the hell brings you here?"

"Friendship, Buddy. Pure friendship. You and Raven garnered a little attention last night." He seated himself without being invited.

Clint shifted the ice bag. "So?"

"So Raven knows too much about your little project. Did you back off like you said you would?"

"Shit, yes. Don't hassle me right now, Pete." He leaned forward to take a sip of his drink and a slight groan escaped his lips.

Pete studied him carefully. "I think you're lying to me, Clint. Remember, I know you as well as anybody, better than anyone else around here."

"You son-of-a-bitch!" Clint roused up in his chair. "I don't have to take that shit from anybody!

Not anybody! Not even you!" He fell back as the exertion shot an intense renewal of pain through his head.

Pete stood over him. "I don't know why I keep bothering with a self-absorbed bastard like you. You think things over. If you come to your senses and want to hear what I have to say before you read it in the tabs, give me a call." He dropped the key on the coffee table and walked out, closing the door softly behind him.

Clint's rage evaporated as quickly as it came. The throbbing in his head began to ease off again as he became calmer. Immediately he regretted his clash with Pete. When the pain had sufficiently lessened Clint swallowed his pride and picked up the phone.

Just as he had decided his friend had not gone directly home Pete answered.

"Pete, I'm sorry. Come back and tell me the worst."

Knowing what a tremendous effort it must have taken for Clint to make an apology Pete responded like the true friend he was. "Give me an hour. I need to take care of a few things."

"I'm not going anywhere."

Clint shuffled across the room to answer Pete's ring. "Your key is right on the table where you left it. Be sure to get it before you go." Clint staggered over to the chair. "I can't remember when a morning after has been this bad."

"One of these days maybe you'll learn not to mix your poisons," Pete suggested.

"I doubt it. Now tell me what's up."

"Whatever you drank last night brought out your most abrasive talents. You pissed everyone off. Ethan, Mandy Meyer, Raven of course, Robert, Harvey, Steve, at least a half-dozen others, even Joey."

"Raven I can understand. I even know what we fought about. But the others? Why are they complaining?"

"Some way or another you managed to slip a barb into everything you said to everyone. You need some friends at this point, Clint. That wasn't very smart."

"What the hell do you expect me to do about it now?"

"For one thing you could restrain yourself enough to avoid pissing me off, too."

Clint felt fury boiling up inside him but repressed the urge to vent his anger. He reminded himself that Pete had come out of concern, not spite.

"Okay. So what do I do?"

"If you'll accept some advice, here's my recommendation. Hold up for a while. Keep a low profile. Do some writing. You always have several ideas stored up. Develop one of them. Stay out of everyone's way until they all cool off. By that time your screenplay will be ready to pitch. Above all quit harassing your Midwestern critic."

Seeing the malice flicker in the director's eyes

Pete added, "You could even take a vocabulary-building course."

Clint swore under his breath but restrained his outburst.

"You're probably right," he admitted. "Not about the vocabulary, but it might be a good idea for me to stay out of sight and write. One story has been playing in my mind lately. It's a fairly hot topic, too. Not stalking," he assured Pete hurriedly.

Pete grinned. "Why not? You have the experience now. Seriously, you have given that up, haven't you?" Then before Clint could answer, he held up his hand and declared, "No. Don't tell me. I don't want to know."

"I'd like to update you," Clint said with uncharacteristic quietness.

"You're still at it?"

"Only the phone calls. No more letters."

Pete glared at his friend without comment.

"I called her last night after I left Joey's. I was angry at the world and wanted to hurt somebody and she was the easiest target." He seemed almost sheepish.

"Did you use the phone here?"

"No. I drove down the coast and stopped at some little bar on the side of the road. There was a pay phone in a real old-fashioned booth in the back. The worst thing is that the bartender heard me. He thought I was fighting with my girlfriend. I don't exactly how much of the conversation he heard but any was too much."

"Conversation? She talked to you? You did

more than phone and hang up?"

"Yeah, I really screwed up. The bitch hung up on me and I lost it. I called her back and . . ."

"You made two calls from the same phone? What if she's having those calls traced? What if the bartender remembers the incident? Clint, you may be in deep shit."

"I know. That's why I took to your suggestion so readily. It might be best if I withdraw for a while. When people ask why, I'll be in seclusion working on a new project."

"And if Raven persists in asking what the project is? After all, that's the way you described the letters."

"Tell her I'm writing. I really will be."

"Okay. I'm out of here." Pete scooped up the key and left.

CHAPTER 7

Michelle awoke the next morning grateful for a peaceful night and excited over the knowledge that she would at least hear Tom's voice, and maybe even see him again, today.

She was busying herself with things which needed doing around the apartment when the phone rang. Michelle dashed to answer and had the receiver to her ear before recalling that it might be the stalker instead of Tom.

"Hello."

"Michelle?" The voice was masculine, neither Lucisi nor the stalker, and it took her a moment to recognize it.

"Hi, Scott."

"What are your plans for this afternoon?"

"Nothing special. Why?"

"Well, I went down to the office yesterday and found a brochure with Shawn's picture in it. I thought I might bring it over."

"Oh, Scott! That would be great! I'd like to show it to Mr. Zachary tomorrow."

"How does between two and two-thirty sound?"

"Fine. I'll be here."

Before she could walk across the room the phone sounded again.

This time she recognized the voice she wanted to hear.

"Michelle?"

"Hi, Tom."

"Did he call?"

"No. It was all quiet here last night."

"Good. Have you been out this morning?"

"Not really. I got the newspaper, but it was right at the door."

"Did you look around when you had the door open? Was the Ford in the parking lot?"

"I didn't notice."

Lucisi withheld comment. Civilians never seemed to learn the importance of constant awareness.

"Tom?" Michelle broke the silence. "Are you there?"

"Yeah. Do you plan to stay home today?"

"I have some company coming over this afternoon. If I go out he'll be with me." Michelle cringed as she realized she had identified her visitor as male. Well, it might not hurt to let Tom know she hadn't been sitting around waiting for him to come along.

"Just as long as he's not a nondescript blond and if you go out you pay attention to whomever gets close to you. Okay?"

"Okay."

"I'll be out this afternoon but you can call me tonight if anything disturbing should occur."

"I will."

Scott arrived shortly after two and promptly handed Michelle the folder. She flipped it open, stopping Scott as he started to point out the picture of his coworker.

"Let me see if I can pick him out. Yesterday Angie noticed a man staring at us. I want to know if he was the one." She perused the brochure checking each picture. "The man from the restaurant isn't here."

"I'm glad to hear that." Scott turned a page and indicated a photograph. "This is Shawn."

"I don't remember meeting him. If you don't mind I'll keep this and show it to Mr. Zachary though. The man who was here and the one at Martinelli's aren't necessarily the same person."

"Fine. Are you free now? It's a beautiful day out. Let's go over to the park and watch some of the charity tennis tournament being played this weekend. By now we should get to see part of the finals."

"Sounds like fun. Give me a few minutes to get ready."

When Michelle and Scott arrived at the park their eyes took in a sea of people.

"Looks like a bigger turnout than they expected," Scott commented. "I'll ask if any tickets are left. He left Michelle at the car and pushed his way to the information table.

Michelle gazed around her, suddenly remembering what Lucisi had said about awareness of those near her. Her heart skipped a beat as a man bumped against her. Then she felt foolish when she saw his brown hair and the two children hanging onto him. As soon as Scott returned she would inform him concerning what the detective told her about the importance of staying together. Michelle opened the door and slid back into the car. She would feel safer inside. It seemed that Scott had been gone forever before she finally saw him working his way back through the crowd.

He was shaking his head regretfully. "No tickets left. What else would you like to do? The day is too pretty to waste."

"Let's go to the zoo. I haven't been there in ages and they have some new animals."

Scott smiled. "Why not? We'll be kids again."

The glorious weather had brought a flock of humanity to the zoo. On the trip over Michelle had briefed Scott as to the detective's cautions and he took her hand as they crossed the parking area.

They were admiring the big cats when Michelle caught a glimpse of a now-familiar figure strolling through the crowd. She nudged Scott and made a comment, then the couple turned to watch as Tom Lucisi, a child clinging to each hand, approached. His attention was devoted to the children and the trio had almost reached them before recognition hit him.

"Hey, Michelle. Great day to be out, isn't it?" Before she could respond he continued, "I'd like you to meet my niece and nephew, Teresa and Tommy Crocetti. Kids, say hello to Miss Wilson."

Michelle acknowledged the children and made her own introduction. "Tom, this is Scott McMillan. Scott, Tom Lucisi."

The men shook hands and the detective asked, "Any sign of your blond admirer?"

Michelle shook her hand. "Nobody. Maybe he won't come back. I'm tired of this already."

"I can't believe someone is after Michelle," Scott remarked. "It's sounds more like something in a novel or a movie."

"It happens though. She'll just have to be careful until we catch him. And we will." Lucisi smiled confidently. "I can feel it."

By this time Teresa was tugging on her uncle's hand. "Come on, Uncle Tommy. I want to see the monkeys. You promised."

Lucisi chuckled. "You can tell who's in charge. Okay, Miss Teri, let's go." They said their farewells and parted.

Clint awakened Sunday morning feeling better and ready to put pen to paper. His writing technique left a great deal to be desired. He scribbled on legal pads, adding and subtracting in the wide margins he allowed until no one - not even Clint himself - could be counted on to interpret the text correctly. Unfortunately he tended to blame whichever friend had agreed to do the typing for all misinterpretations, causing many delays in his finished products.

After a scant breakfast Clint sat on the floor by the coffee table (his favorite writing position) and began a short synopsis of the plot.

Midafternoon Clint stood up and stretched, wiggling the muscles in his stiff back. He had written steadily and the script was flowing as easily as if someone were standing at his side telling him the story. Hunger gnawed at his stomach. Yesterday food had not appealed to him and today he had been too involved to stop for nourishment. What Clint wanted now was a steak dinner and a massage. He reflected ruefully that rubs from Raven would no longer be forthcoming. At least the steak was readily available.

Soon he was sitting in a small nearby cafe with a steaming cup of coffee in front of him. Clint had considered, then decided against, inviting anyone to join him. He hated to eat alone but he had been unable to think of anyone who would be sympathetic company. Even conversation with Pete would have been a strain at this point. The waitress placed a heaping plate of steak and potatoes in front of him and he wiped his mind clear of brooding and concentrated on the food.

Finally satisfied he signaled the waitress for the check. Clint felt good. Leaving a generous tip, he rose and went to the register to pay.

The late afternoon sun was warm on his back as he walked to his car. The idea of a short drive occurred to him and Clint turned away from home as he pulled into the street. As he drove he mulled over his screenplay-in-progress. It would make a box office hit for sure. Just as well he had not taken a shot at a stalker story.

That thought brought his own project, as he insisted on calling it, to mind. Clint still had no intention of giving up the phone calls. A pay phone beckoned to him from a shopping area. Unable to resist he pulled in beside it and began to fish coins from his pocket only to discover the phone had been vandalized. Clint swore under his breath and got back into the car.

Three damaged phones later he decided fate did not intend for him to make a call tonight. Tomorrow, as Scarlett O'Hara had said, would be another day. Time enough to continue his long-distance harassment.

Ann Snuggs

CHAPTER 8

It was after nine when Michelle's phone sounded. Glancing at the display and ascertaining the identity of her caller she answered with confidence.

"Hello, Tom."

"How did . . . . Oh, you looked at your Caller ID."

"You bet. I really like this. I like knowing who's calling before you pick up the phone."

She heard Tom's warm laugh at the other end of the line. "You should make a commercial."

"Maybe so. No one has called except people I know. The message indicator was flashing when we got home but both the numbers were friends. No strangers."

"Good."

"Your niece and nephew are cute. Are they twins? They look about the same age."

"They're eighteen months apart. Tommy is six. Teresa will be five next month. They're my sister Carla's kids."

"Do you babysit often?"

"My chances are limited because of my job but I try to spend time with Tommy at least once a month. He's my namesake and my godson."

"That's nice of you."

"It's my responsibility. I take my responsibilities seriously.

"Did you pay attention to what was happening around you this afternoon?" Tom changed the subject.

"Aye, aye, sir," responded Michelle, half-provoked, half-joking.

Lucisi ignored her tone. "Any sign of blond men? Remember, we still are not sure what he looks like."

"No one close enough to me to stand out. Scott helped me watch."

"Well, tomorrow I have to testify in court so if you need anything call my partner, Mike Fitzgerald. He's the blond man whose desk is by mine. I'll update him before I head to the courthouse."

"Great. Then I'll get to harass a blond man."

Lucisi laughed. "I doubt that he would consider your call that. Mike's a good guy."

"I was a witness several months ago. It was an interesting experience."

"What was the case? The perpetrator wasn't by any chance blond, was he?"

"Actually it was a she. I just happened to be one of a half-dozen people in a booth by the register when she tried to rob the cafe we were in. The deputy prosecutor asked me to testify because he said that, in his opinion, I would appear as a credible witness.

"I believe that. Who was the prosecutor?"

"Earl, no, Eric Pedersen, a real no-personality. Oops! I shouldn't have said that. Do you know him?"

"Not well. I know who he is. If I saw him outside of business he'd probably have to identify himself for me."

"Well, I'm not sure I'd know him again either. He doesn't have a powerful presence. You'd think he would need one for his job, wouldn't you?"

"I guess. Just remember to call Detective Fitzgerald if anything comes up tomorrow, okay?"

"Fine. Have fun in court."

"Oh, yeah. It's my favorite thing." Sarcasm dripped from Lucisi's words. "You be careful and watch what's happening around you."

"I will."

Michelle was a bit disappointed that Tom had not mentioned seeing her again but she shrugged it off and decided to make an early night of it.

That Sunday afternoon the blond man had taken his time getting to Michelle's apartment. Once again he left the car several blocks away and made his approach on foot. This was often Michelle's day in and more than once he had spent his time watching the closed door and catching brief glances of his desired woman only when she moved near the windows.

This day his opportunity to see her more fully came about mid-afternoon when Scott arrived and then escorted Michelle out of the apartment. The stalker practically ran to retrieve his car and was gratified to see Scott's car passing his as he slid into the driver's seat. He gave them an extended lead then caught up with Michelle and Scott as they turned on to the boulevard that led to the park.

The watcher easily lost himself in the crowd that milled around the area of the tennis matches and was able to keep an eye on Michelle without her suspecting his presence. He noticed that his adored one seemed edgy. Her nervousness was obvious to one who observed her so carefully. When Scott and Michelle discussed the zoo the stalker was close enough to hear and actually beat them to their destination.

Becoming invisible among the people who strolled along the paths between the cages and animal housing compounds was a snap and the blond man followed every movement of Michelle and Scott throughout the afternoon.

He frowned at the sight of Lucisi greeting them then immediately was swept by relief. The dark man had two children in tow, ones who bore a physical resemblance to him. Perhaps he was married and a close friend of Michelle or the woman who was with them the night before. It was a comforting thought. Nevertheless he would still check out the license plate number.

    Late that night Michelle's obsessed admirer lay in his bed and dreamed of holding her close. He could almost feel the softness of her skin beneath his fingers, the warmth of her lips crushed by his own. His imaginings overwhelmed him and he groaned aloud. This couldn't go on. He must find a way to possess her soon.

Ann Snuggs

CHAPTER 9

After the activity of the weekend the regular crises of Monday morning at work seemed dull. Michelle was edgy about phone calls but by noon, with no word from her stalker, she had begun to relax.

In the afternoon she had several appointments and things were rolling along so smoothly that she started looking for something to go wrong. "Silly," she chided herself.

It was almost five when the call she had been dreading came through.

"Michelle?"

"Yes."

"You shouldn't hang up on people. It shows bad manners."

Chills ran through her and Michelle wished that she had taken at least one of her co-workers into her confidence.

"So does calling people at two in the morning," responded Michelle tartly.

"Now, Michelle, you shouldn't talk to your friends like that." The threat in Clint's smooth, caressing tone aroused a flood of sudden anger in Michelle.

"You're not my friend and never will be," she snapped and quickly broke the connection.

Only minutes later Michelle was walking out the door when Judy hailed her from the front desk. "This call's for you."

"Take a message, please. I'm late for an appointment," she lied.

Clint chuckled as he hung up the phone. His second day of creativity had mellowed him and taken the edge off his usually hair-trigger temper. He had her on the run. It was obvious from the panicked way she had flared at him that the calls were unnerving her. It was probable that she had told the receptionist to say she was out. Actually the bitch was shivering at her desk Clint told himself with a smile.

The phone call made him feel so good that Clint decided to take a shot at smoothing things over with Raven. He stopped at another pay phone and made the call. The answering machine picked up on the fifth ring. Clint waited for the tone then changed his mind and hung up. No message would be sufficient. He could try later - if he was still in the mood.

Clint returned to his apartment and his story but was unable to progress. The work had already consumed close to seven hours of his day and solitude was not Clint's favorite condition. He was sociable by nature in spite of his inordinate talent for rubbing people the wrong way. Two days of his own company had left him restless. He picked up the phone.

This time Raven answered. Clint could feel iciness radiating across the phone line when she recognized his voice. Only the desire for the touch of her hands on his aching shoulders kept him from tossing an insult at her and hanging up.

"Still mad at me?" he inquired in his most velvet tone.

"I'm not mad, I just don't want anything to do with an animal like you."

"Maybe you'd be interested in stroking the savage beast."

"I can't imagine why."

This was going to be more difficult than Clint had anticipated.

"Come on, Raven. You know I think you're terrific."

"It's too bad I can't say the same about you."

"Just have dinner with me tonight so I can see your pretty face."

"Clint, that line of bullshit has always irritated me and you damn well know it."

"Well, you name the time. At least have the frigging courtesy to say this shit to my face."

Raven chose a day and Clint hung up quickly, before his sharp tongue got away from him.

Michelle entered her apartment and called to Sultan. She dropped the usual pile of mail of the table and went to the bedroom to scratch the cat and change clothes. As she opened the top drawer of the dresser she noticed an earring on the floor. "That's odd," she said to Sultan, who had curled on a bed pillow to watch her. "I don't ever leave my jewelry in your reach. Since you can't open drawers, how did this get out?"

Sultan responded with a piercing gaze that, of course, told her nothing.

Michelle opened a drawer and took out her jewelry box. She frowned when she raised the lid. Her careful placement system had been disturbed. She was sure everything had been in its proper place this morning. When she had put the key in the lock only a short time before the door had been securely closed. How on earth could someone have accessed the box to leave it in disorder?

Well, the first thing was to determine if anything was missing. Sitting on the bed with the jewelry box in front of her Michelle began to empty it, mentally inventorying each piece. When everything had been removed only the mate to the earring on the floor was gone.

Michelle sat and bit her lip and thought. Was

it possible that she herself in hurrying to get ready this morning had forgotten and left the pair out? Sultan would certainly have discovered her slip and taken advantage. But she would not have messed up the contents of the box. Someone else must have been in the apartment.

With a flash of clairvoyance MIchelle suddenly knew - not supposed or reasoned - that a stranger had been here and the realization that he had been going through her place touching her things sent ice through her. Shivering violently she grabbed the phone.

The switchboard operator had answered before Michelle remembered that Tom had gone to court and it took her a second to recall the blond detective's name.

"Fitzgerald."

"Detective Fitzgerald, this is Michelle Wilson. Detective Lucisi told me I could call you if something happened while he was in court and . . ."

Mike broke in before she could finish. "Lucisi just walked in about five minutes ago. Hold on." He put his hand over the phone.

"Hey, Tom. Did you tell someone to ask for me if you weren't available? Female, of course."

"Yeah, my stalker lady. Did she call?"

Mike gestured with the receiver. "She's calling now and sounds kind of shaky."

Lucisi snatched up his phone. "Michelle? What's wrong?"

Hearing the comforting sound of Tom's voice, Michelle almost sobbed with relief. The way being stalked had shattered her confidence amazed her. "Someone has been in my apartment. I can feel it."

The detective smiled but kept his tone serious. "Do you have proof? You didn't go in again with the door open?"

"No. It was locked when I got home but my jewelry box had been rifled and an earring is missing. Tom, I'm scared."

"Keep the door locked and sit tight. I'll be there as soon as I can."

Fitzgerald gave Tom a questioning look.

"Someone is really playing with this girl's mind," Lucisi commented. "I'll finish this paperwork in the morning. I'm going to check on her now."

Mike grinned. "And what part of her are you playing with?" he teased.

"No part - yet," Tom answered with a twinkle in his eye. "But I'm working on it."

Michelle was pacing the floor waiting impatiently for Tom to arrive when the phone rang. She considered letting it ring then remembered the Caller ID. The area code was unfamiliar. She gripped the receiver firmly, took a deep breath and answered by demanding, "Where are you?"

Silence greeted her from the other end of the line.

"Where are you?" Michelle repeated.

The sound of a soft click greeted her ears as Clint hung up.

As she returned the phone to its base the

doorbell rang and she flew to answer. A quick glance through the peephole told her that Tom had arrived. She threw the door open.

"I'm really glad you're here," Michelle said in a tone that reinforced her words.

Lucisi went straight to the point. "When did you discover you were invaded?"

Michelle smiled faintly. "What an appropriate term, 'invaded'. That's just the way I feel."

"Most people who have break-ins do feel violated. It's common." Not sure how the gesture would be received, Tom restrained himself from putting a comforting arm around her and repeated, "When did you find out?"

"After I got home from work. I was opening a dresser drawer and looked down. An earring was lying on the floor at my feet. I took out my jewelry box to put it back and noticed everything in the box had been shuffled around. I took inventory and the only thing missing was the other earring like this." Michelle held out the piece she had retrieved from the floor.

Lucisi took it and examined it carefully. "It doesn't look expensive."

"It's not. Just moderately-priced costume jewelry. Anyway, nothing else was gone. Why would anyone want a single earring?"

"This one was on the floor. I suspect whoever was here thought he had both of them. Have you checked the rest of the apartment? Was anything else disturbed or taken?"

"I don't know. The idea of someone going

through my things upset me so that I just waited for you." Michelle turned her blue eyes up to his dark ones with a trust that caused Tom to forget restraint and pull her into the circle of his arms.

"Don't worry," he assured her. "I'll find this guy and get him off the streets."

"Something else. I got another call."

"Here or at the office?"

"Both."

"Then we should have a number on the one that came here." He crossed to check the display.

"I looked before I answered. It's out of state. I don't recognize the area code."

Lucisi glanced at the number. "Somewhere around L.A." A puzzled frown settled on his face. "How could someone break into this apartment and call you from California in the same day? It doesn't make sense."

He took Michelle's hand, led her into the living room and pulled her down beside him on the sofa.

"There's always air travel," she suggested.

"True, but it seems a bit unbelievable."

They sat close together without conversation for several minutes then Tom spoke. "Let's do this. I'll inspect all the possible points of entry to your apartment and try to determine where and how he got in. You examine the drawers and closets to see if anything else is out of order or missing. When we finish I'll take you to dinner. Okay?"

"All right," Michelle agreed.

Their efforts produced nothing. No sign of

forced entry was evident nor did Michelle find any other disruption. Even the day's mail was benign, no threatening letters.

They reached Martinelli's as the bulk of the dinner crowd was leaving and were seated without a wait. It had been easy for Tom to persuade Michelle to return to the restaurant. She loved the food there and was curious about Tom's family. She hoped the evening would present the opportunity to meet his aunt.

Her hopes were fulfilled even before the salads arrived. A short, dark lady came to the table. Lucisi rapidly rose to his feet and hugged her. "Aunt Teresa, I want you to meet Michelle Wilson. You might say she's a client of mine.

"Michelle this is Mrs. Rossini, my aunt."

"I'm pleased to meet you, Mrs. Rossini." Michelle offered her hand.

Tom's Aunt Teresa took Michelle's hand in both of hers. "It's I who am pleased to see you." She reached up and patted the embarrassed detective's cheek affectionately. "My Tommy doesn't get out enough. It's always work, work, work."

"Now, Aunt Teresa." Lucisi's face was beginning to show color.

"Where did you meet such a pretty girl, Tommy? Surely not dealing with criminals."

It was Michelle's turn to blush crimson. "Mrs. Rossini, you flatter me."

"Michelle is a victim, Aunt Teresa. Someone is threatening her."

"Who would do such a thing?" Mrs. Rossini

shook her head sadly. "So many bad things happen today."

"We don't know who yet, Aunt Teresa, and I'm trying to cheer her up so let's talk about something else."

Michelle picked up the ball and ran with it. "Yes, Mrs. Rossini, let's talk about the wonderful food you serve here. It's always a treat for me to come to Martinelli's. Do you ever share your recipes?"

Aunt Teresa's eyes sparkled. "Only with very special people. What is your favorite dish? Someday I may share it with you. Of course, you would have to make it with me. My recipes are not written down."

The conversation continued along light lines until the salads were brought and Mrs. Rossini excused herself.

When she had disappeared into the kitchen, Michelle turned to Tom and asked, "Was she serious about not writing down her recipes? Surely she doesn't make everything herself."

Lucisi laughed. "Aunt Teresa is quite a kidder. That was her way of saying she wanted to know you better. When I was a kid she taught all of us to cook and along the way learned our hopes and dreams. Her kitchen seemed magic to Carla and me. That was before she opened the restaurant."

"Can you really make some of these wonderful dishes? I'm impressed!"

"Well, mine don't necessarily taste like hers but I can stir up a few company meals."

"I'd like to have one sometime," Michelle declared boldly.

Tom flashed one of his most enchanting smiles. "It's a deal. I'll hold you to it."

Before they had gone to eat Lucisi had put in a call to check out the California number and, upon reaching Michelle's apartment and seeing the station number on the display, he phoned in to learn the location from which the call had come.

"The pay phone is at a busy intersection," he informed her after a short conversation. "It could be anybody."

Michelle patted the sofa cushion beside her and Tom sat down.

"If your aunt is Mrs. Rossini, why is the restaurant Martinelli's?"

Tom gave a surprised chuckle. "Well, that question certainly came out of the blue. Aunt Teresa didn't want to use her own name. She picked Martinelli out of a novel."

"Oh. That seems like an odd way to name a restaurant."

"It was logical to her. My aunt thinks in a unique manner. She's very special. Carla's Teresa, the little girl you met, is her namesake."

"Like Tommy is yours? Your family seems to be close."

"We are. You've never mentioned yours."

"No, I haven't," Michelle said in a tone that closed the door.

Lucisi glanced at his watch. "I need to be going. Do you feel all right about staying here alone? Could you ask Angie to stay with you or maybe go to her place?"

"I'm fine. When you leave I'll lock the deadbolt. Though they give me the creeps the phone calls can't actually hurt me."

"Okay. Call me before you leave for work in the morning. I'll be at the station early."

"I will."

After he hung up Clint stood for a moment with his hand still on the phone. Why had Michelle asked for his location? He needed to think this through completely before proceeding. On the drive home he concentrated on the way Michelle's voice had sounded. He replayed her words in his mind.

By the time Clint reached his apartment he believed he had the solution. Michelle had found a method of determining the number of the phones he was using. Of course. How simple could it be? She had Caller ID. The phone companies were promoting the service heavily. He would have to be very careful to use each phone only once. Having the number of pay phones throughout the area would do her no good.

The idea flitted through his mind that perhaps she had notified the police but he dismissed it out of hand. Even a bitch who didn't have the intelligence to appreciate his films would have enough sense to recognize a joke. Nevertheless he needed to use extreme caution when he made the calls.

The stalker stood in his bedroom and searched his pockets for the fourth time. Where was the mate to the dangling piece of silver he held in his hand? He swore out loud. It must have fallen as he slipped his hand into the pocket. Now it would become obvious to Michelle that someone had been in her apartment.
Michelle. What a lovely name.
The man knew women. If both earrings were missing Michelle would assume she herself had misplaced them. With only one gone . . . . He shook his head ruefully. It was critical that he remain invisible and unknown. He could not afford to be seen and recognized. Even the rumor of such an impropriety and his career would be destroyed. He cursed himself again for his carelessness. Today would have to be his last visit to the apartment for some time.
After eating, the blond man settled in his bed and drew from under the pillow the nightgown he had taken from Michelle's apartment the previous week. He pulled it closely against his body and stroked it. Continuing to caress the garment he opened a book and began to read.

Ann Snuggs

CHAPTER 10

Lucisi was working on the last form in his stack when Mike Fitzgerald dropped a bag bulging with doughnuts on the desk beside the typewriter.

"Was last night worth the early morning?" Mike asked with a grin.

"Oh, yeah. This might be the one."

"Seems like I've heard that before."

"Yeah, well, this one's different."

"Have a doughnut and tell me about her in twenty-five words or less," Mike invited.

Lucisi pulled a sugary morsel from the bag and took a bite before answering. "I'd rather talk about this stalker. He doesn't make sense. Yesterday Michelle found an earring lying on the floor when she got home from work. She is confident that it was in the jewelry box when she left the apartment. I examined every conceivable means of access and found absolutely no trace of entry."

"Maybe she just forgot she had left out the earrings."

"Possible but not probable. She's very organized.

"Anyway that's not the most puzzling part. Yesterday afternoon around five-thirty her Caller ID recorded the number of a pay phone in the Los Angeles area. How could the stalker take an earring here and make a call from L.A.?"

"Ever heard of flying?"

"Sure, but . . .. I don't know. I feel like I'm missing something."

"Maybe it's a conspiracy," suggested Fitzgerald jokingly. "What does this Michelle do?"

"She sells real estate. There's a thought. I'll have to ask if she's had any clients coming from or going to the West Coast."

Just then Captain Barkley appeared by Lucisi's desk. "You fellows need to take this call." He handed Fitzgerald a piece of paper and Lucisi grabbed his coat. The detectives began another busy day.

It was late afternoon when Tom finally caught a chance to check with Michelle. She was out but he left the message for her to return his call.

It was almost eight o'clock when their game of phone tag finally connected them.

"At last," Michelle answered when she saw

Tom's number displayed. "You're a hard man to catch."

Tom laughed heartily and Michelle could picture his smiling face. "Just how do you mean that?"

Michelle was embarrassed. "You know what I mean. I called you off and on all day and both you and Detective Fitzgerald were out each time."

"Yeah. It's been a full one.

"Any calls?" Tom changed the subject. "Any blond men in evidence?"

"No to both questions. No exciting mail either."

"Good. Maybe he'll give us a day to catch our breath. The California call still intrigues me. Mike wondered if you had had any recent business deals which involved people coming or going west. Have you?"

"None that immediately come to mind but I'll check my records tomorrow."

"Michelle, who have you told about this?"

"Only a few close friends. You've met Angie and Scott. Judy Austen who handles the switchboard at the office knows, but I haven't mentioned it to anyone else at work. Mr. Johnson, the manager here. You met him, too. He probably told Mr. Zachary. I find the situation uncomfortable to discuss. The people I have told may have talked about it. I don't know. Why? Does it matter who knows?"

"Probably not. However, if the stalker thinks we're on to him, he may back off."

"That sounds good to me."

"In a way, yes. Although it could keep us from ever identifying him. In the long run I'd rather know who he is."

"Me, too," Michelle agreed.

"Are you okay for tonight? If so, it's been a long day and I'll hit the sack. If you want me to, I'll come over."

Michelle could hear the exhaustion in Tom's tone and in spite of her wish to see him she assured him of her safety.

Detective Lucisi was very much on Michelle's mind as she half-heartedly thumbed through a magazine. When the phone rang she absent-mindedly picked it up without bothered to notice its source.

"Hello."

"Good evening, Michelle." The softly threatening sound of Clint's voice caused her heart to jerk. Her eyes flicked to the display box only to be greeted by the word, "anonymous."

"Clever of you to try to locate me," Clint continued. "Clever of me to figure it out. I'm proud of us both."

Without giving her time to respond, Clint whispered, "Later, Michelle," and broke the connection.

Michelle fought back the overwhelming desire to dial Tom's number. She reminded herself that phone calls could do her no real harm, especially if they were initiating in California. The same thing baffled her that had perplexed Lucisi. How did the long distance calls fit in with the man who hovered in the shadows here? The thought that suddenly flared in her mind was too absurd to be taken seriously. Could two men be involved? If so, were they working together or by some fantastic coincidence were two separate men stalking her?

Sultan strolled up and leapt into her lap for his nightly attention. She cuddled him against her and he began to purr.

"What do you think, Sultan? Personally, I believe we have slipped into the Twilight Zone." She lifted the Persian's chin and looked him squarely in the eye. "We'll suggest that to Tom tomorrow." The cat pulled from her grasp and jumped from her lap with a yowl.

Michelle laughed at him and ran her fingers down his tail causing him to swat at her hand.

"You haven't decided to accept Tom, have you? Adjust, Sultan. I think Detective Lucisi may be a keeper."

In spite of the idea of two stalkers playing through Michelle's mind she slept well and awoke early wondering if Tom was stirring yet. She could hardly wait to throw the possibility of separate entities at him, although she feared he might receive her theory with laughter. Michelle hated to be laughed at.

By waiting until after seven-thirty she almost

missed him.

"Tom, I need to see you today."

"What happened? Are you all right?"

"I'm fine. Something occurred to me last night. I want to know what you think of the idea."

"Can we talk tonight? I was on my way out the door."

"Sure. What time?"

"I'll call you later."

Clint wrote rapidly and was more than halfway through his first draft when his doorbell rang Tuesday afternoon. He rose and started across the room but stopped when he heard the key in the lock.

"Is it safe to enter?" Pete greeted him cheerfully. "I see from the looks of the place your writing is going well." He gestured to the pages strewn around on the floor.

"Damn straight. I can't believe how smoothly it's flowing."

Pete selected a page at random and scanned it. "It's flowing a little too smoothly. Who in the hell can read this? I'll bet you can't yourself."

"Don't be such an encouraging son-of-a-bitch, Pete. When I rewrite it'll be plainer."

"Sure. How about a drink? Do you have anything I like in the place?"

"Probably not. Look for yourself. And while you're at it fix something for me." Clint returned to his interrupted work.

"Thanks," he said as Pete handed him a glass. "Give me ten minutes to finish this thought and we can go somewhere for lunch. Why don't you call for reservations?"

An hour later they were settled at a table talking over drinks while they waited for their food.

"I talked to Raven yesterday," commented Clint. "She's still pissed at me."

"Well, at least she's speaking. Or did she slam the phone down in your ear?"

"Close. Raven can be such a bitch. If she wasn't so damn satisfying I'd write her off. She was really snotty about getting together but finally agreed to Thursday night."

"Wasn't she pleased to hear you're giving up your terrorist campaign?"

Clint shrugged. "I guess."

Something in Clint's manner told Pete that his friend was lying to him - again. He stared at the director searchingly. "But, of course, you really haven't. Don't bother to deny it. I read you like a book."

Clint remained silent but rage blazed in his eyes.

"Don't give me that look either. I have no intention of telling anyone, Raven included." Pete shook his head reprovingly. "If you don't have enough sense to quit on your own it's your problem."

Clint's angry retort was postponed by the appearance of the waiter with their meal.

"Will there be anything else?" he inquired

solicitously.

"This is fine. Thanks, Eddie," responded Pete.

"You really piss me off with your damned self-righteous attitude. Who the hell do you think you are?" Clint demanded fiercely when Eddie was out of earshot.

"Your pal. Drop it, Clint. Just forget it. You won't listen to reason anyway."

The heavy silence at the table was palpable. Neither man spoke until the meal was almost finished. Clint was wisely letting his wrath abate before replying and Pete had nothing left to say.

"I did give up the letters," Clint conceded.

"Good." Pete was unmoved.

"Don't push me, Pete."

"I've said everything I'm going to say. When the shit hits the fan I won't even say, 'I told you so.'"

Eddie returned to ask about a dessert order and the conversation stopped. Pete declined but Clint requested a chocolate and ice cream confection.

"Glad to see your tantrum didn't affect your appetite," Pete commented dryly.

Clint chuckled wryly. "If I'm going to jail like you keep predicting I'd better eat fancy food while I can. My sense of humor wasn't affected either."

Pete relented and broke into laughter. "Clint you entertain the hell out of me. No matter what kind of pain in the ass you are, you are so damn funny."

His friend's merriment was reflected in Clint's

face. "It's good to know you appreciate my true worth."

When Pete dropped Clint at his apartment, the director started for his door but veered toward his car as soon as his friend disappeared from sight. It was time for his daily call to Michelle.

Ann Snuggs

CHAPTER 11

Fortunately for Tom's frame of mind as well as the opportunity to make connections with Michelle, his work day was calmer than the previous one. As they had agreed, Michelle was waiting for him when he and Mike came out of the building.

Michelle recognized them and pulled her car to the entrance, admiring the figure Lucisi presented when he stopped to say something to his partner. Well-built and dark with poise stemming from self-confidence, his coat casually thrown across his arm, the detective reminded her of a man in a magazine ad.

Turning away from Fitzgerald, Tom saw her and waved. He ran easily down the steps and opened the car door she unlocked for him.

"Your car or mine?" he asked. "Make it light on yourself. Whichever one we leave will be okay here."

"Get in," she invited. "I'll be your chauffeur - or should I say chauffeuress?"

"Call it whatever you want as long as you take me where I want to go."

"And where might that be, sir?" she said breezily.

Tom reacted to her cheeriness with a smile and good humor of his own. "Home, James."

"Oh, dear!" Michelle exclaimed in mock-horror. "He's taken leave of his senses and forgotten my name."

Lucisi burst into laughter. "You certainly are in a good mood this evening. Did anything special happen?"

"No. Actually nothing happened today except business-as-usual and it's been such a relief that I'm giddy.

"Where are we going really?" she finished.

"To my home Really. I'm going to cook for you."

Michelle raised an eyebrow and glanced at him sideways. "Sounds intriguing. How do I get there?"

Easily following Lucisi's explicit directions Michelle soon pulled into the driveway of an older duplex.

Tom turned the key in the lock and ushered Michelle into an old-fashioned entry hall. "This belongs to a friend of my father's. Some kind of distant cousin, I think. It's not stylish but it's sufficient for my needs."

"What an interesting decor," commented Michelle as she stepped into a living room full of furniture from another time period complete with doilies on the tables and antimacassars on the horsehair sofa and chairs. The components of Tom's modern sound and video systems were interspersed wherever space allowed, intrusive as obscenities at a ladies' tea party.

Lucisi shrugged. "It works for me. Would you like to watch the news or listen to music while I get things started in the kitchen?"

"I'd rather observe your culinary techniques. Or do you allow sightseers?"

Tom favored her with one of his magnificent smiles. "No secrets. You can follow my every move."

Entering the kitchen was like traveling to another dwelling. Everything spoke of constant use and care. It was devoid of gadgetry but well-worn utensils and appliances were placed conveniently for both preparation and eating.

Michelle looked around appreciatively as Lucisi pulled out a chair by the table and gestured for her to sit.

"This is marvelous."

"It's the only room I live in on a regular basis. My job keeps me too involved to do much at home besides eat and sleep. I like to eat and, since I also enjoy cooking, I spend the majority of my time here."

"Then how come all you had for lunch last

Saturday was beer and snacks?"

Tom chuckled and shook his head. "Wouldn't you pick up on that discrepancy? I worked late and didn't get up and out early enough to grocery. After I made that nine o'clock call to you I slept until after noon."

"A likely story. But we'll soon find out what kind of a cook you really are. Can I do anything to help?"

"Just sit and tell me what you needed to talk about this morning. Later you can set the table."

Clint slammed down the phone, beginning to lose patience. This was the third call he had made to Michelle with no answer. His awareness of her probable source of tracing caused him to feel obligated to change phones for each call and he was tired of going from pay phone to pay phone. What could the bitch be doing instead of going home? Working late? Clint refused to believe anyone who didn't appreciate his talent could have a life other than work or home. His ego was such that he regarded most of his critics as jealous wanna-bes, needing to revile him because they had no creativity of their own.

An hour later when Michelle still did not answer Clint began to fantasize about the target of his abuse. Maybe Pete was right. Perhaps she was a fan trying to get his attention. He admitted to himself her voice sounded younger than he had expected when he planned the campaign. Maybe she did watch his films. It was even possible that she meant the criticism to be constructive. Clint quickly rejected that thought. His original analysis had to be the correct one. Some self-righteous bitch attacking Hollywood because it was the thing to do. Clint Sharkey was simply a handy butt. He would try the work number.

Decision made, Clint drove to still another pay phone and made the call but no one answered. Where could she be? His desire for the daily sound of her voice was becoming obsessive.

Michelle and Tom arrived at her apartment a little after ten. He had insisted on following her home and seeing her to the door. She had not resisted much.

"Are you coming in?" she invited.

"No, tomorrow's another work day."

"Thank you for a lovely evening. The dinner was delicious. Your cooking is impressive."

"Thank you for the compliment." Tom lifted her chin with his hand and gazed deeply into her eyes. "The flavor was improved by your presence." His lips brushed hers softly then he straightened and became businesslike. "Lock up before I leave. I'll see you tomorrow."

Michelle stood at the window watching Lucisi as he drove off. Her heart was still fluttering in response to the caress of the detective's lips. The gentleness of his touch excited feelings deep within her. She moved dreamily to the bedroom to begin her nightly routine.

Sultan crawled from under the bed and meowed his reproach. She scooped him up and carried him to the kitchen scratching his ears and murmuring to him apologetically. He wiggled from her arms as they reached his feeding station. Michelle opened a can of fancy cat food and dumped it in his bowl.

"Sorry, Sultan. Tonight I was not only feeding my body but also my soul. You'll have to get used to it." She knelt beside the Persian and stroked him as he gobbled her offering.

The ring of the phone snapped her out of her reverie. Michelle strolled to the display box, deciding not to let the caller hurry her. Sure enough, the number was that of a phone on the West Coast. Michelle reached for the phone then suddenly changed her mind. Why should she let some nut disturb her wonderful evening? The call was not from a friend. She resolved to ignore it. After ten rings the sound ceased. Michelle mentally patted herself on the back for her determination and returned to the living room.

Later she lay in bed reliving the enchanting evening. Tom was truly a dream. Michelle was totally enamored of him and believed that he found her attractive, too. She certainly hoped his attentiveness was more than just doing his job. Through a flight of fantasy she felt his lips touching hers again and her imagination expanded the picture to include his strong arms holding her tightly against his body. As Michelle envisioned her arms clasping around his neck the phone rang again jerking her rudely back to reality.

With a flounce she turned on the lamp and stretched to check the Caller ID. Still another West Coast area code. Michelle was sorely tempted to snatch up the receiver and tell off her persistent harasser without even saying hello but she stolidly listened to the steady ringing, having convinced herself that no answer was the best way to handle it. Tom could advise her in the morning. For now she would let it ring.

When the noise finally stopped she recalled Lucisi's reaction to the suggestion of two stalkers. Michelle had expected him to laugh instead of giving it serious consideration. He surprised her by admitting that, unbelievable as it might be at first blush, it would provide a logical explanation to the missing earring at home and the phone call from California on the same day. The frightening side of this solution was that the caller whom she believed had no genuine desire to harm her and the person who had been in her apartment were not one and the same.

Michelle glanced at the clock. After midnight. She firmly put all parts of the puzzle out of her mind, rolled over and went to sleep.

Clint's pique had begun to take on an aura of concern. Where in the hell was his victim? She was always back in her house by this time of night. Surely she hadn't gone off and abandoned him. He left the pay phone and drove home to drink himself to sleep.

The blond man sat and worried. Michelle's new friend was a police detective. He had him identified now. Thomas Lucisi. Had she gone to the police about him? The detective had been with her before his carelessness with the earring. Had Michelle observed him watching her? Careful had been his watchword. His advantage in following her was that he was not the kind of man people notice. A friend might have introduced her to the detective. That would be possible. The man comforted himself with the thought. He held to it tenaciously.

Giving up Michelle had become an impossibility for him. He had to see her, to smell her perfume wafting his direction, to brush against her on the street anonymously, to watch the graceful movement of her body. No. The man could not give up Michelle now, no matter what he had to do to be near her.

CHAPTER 12

When Pete let himself into Clint's apartment the next afternoon he found his friend saturated with alcohol, half-hidden in a cloud of smoke. No evidence of work was in sight.

"Hey, man, what's up? I thought the story was flowing like wine and today all I see is the wine."

"Writer's block," Clint snarled. "And it's gin, not wine."

Pete suppressed a smile knowing out-and-out laughter would do nothing to relieve the director's surly mood. "How about a late lunch to go with drinks? My treat."

Clint scowled at his friend but nodded his agreement.

"Get dressed and we'll go. I'll drive."

As Pete had expected Clint's sullenness dissipated as the meal progressed.

"So talk about your story. Maybe bouncing it off me will break the block," suggested Pete.

Clint shrugged. "I doubt it."

"It's worked in the past."

Clint gave no response. Pete studied him speculatively.

"Something else is on your mind, isn't it? What happened? Did Raven back out on your date?"

"I haven't talked to Raven."

"Whom have you talked to, besides your critic in the boondocks?"

"I haven't talked to her either."

Pete raised a questioning eyebrow. "Don't tell me you've finally come to your senses and dropped it."

Clint paused before blunting out, "She won't answer the frigging phone."

Light dawned for Pete. "Damn, Clint! You and your obsessive personality. You've gotten addicted to these weird phone calls, haven't you?" He threw back his head and laughed. "It serves you right. Sorry. I said I wouldn't gloat when it all came back to bite you."

To his surprise Pete realized that Clint's hair-trigger temper had not flared. The director was still sitting and smoking, staring into space reflectively.

"I need her to finish this damn screenplay, Pete. I need to hear that voice on the edge of panic. She won't frigging answer. How in the hell am I going to get her to pick up the damn phone?"

"I thought you weren't dealing with stalking."

"I'm not. The story does involve psychological torture though." He paused thoughtfully. "I can't believe I just said that. These calls were never intended to inflict any real harm and I just got through admitting to both of us that they could."

"Clint! Don't tell me you've discovered a conscience! Not you!" Pete stared at his friend in amazement.

"Obviously not since I intend to keep up the calling until this screenplay is completely developed. Maybe I'll give the bitch a credit in the titles." He chuckled. "Wouldn't that burn her ass?"

"Who's knows? She might be flattered."

"Not likely. Be a pal. Take me by a pay phone on the way home."

"No way. You harass own your own, Clint, my boy. Leave me out of it. My hands are clean and are going to stay that way."

Pete could tell Clint was angry, but he made no comment on the drive back to his apartment and when they arrived said polite goodbyes and thanked Pete for lunch. Within a matter of minutes afterwards he was in his car cruising to find another pay phone.

Mid-morning Michelle found a pause in her schedule to put in a call for Tom. Surprisingly he was in and had a moment to talk.

"How are you this morning?" he asked. "Any

calls? Any prowlers?"

"Fine. Yes. No. In that order," she responded lightheartedly.

"Where did they originate and what did he say?"

"They were all from California and I didn't answer when I saw the location."

"Interesting decision."

"I felt too good after the evening with you. I wasn't going to allow him to upset me."

Warmth was plain in Lucisi's voice. "I'm glad you enjoyed the evening as much as I did. How about tonight? Your place or mine?"

"At mine you'll probably get KFC."

"I can handle it. What time?"

"Around eight. I have a late appointment to show a house."

"I'll be waiting for you. Be careful running around after dark by yourself. Keep a careful lookout for blond men or anyone else who appears to take a special interest in you."

"Does that include tall, dark detectives?" Michelle teased.

"Most especially tall, dark detectives," he answered in a tone of mock-sincerity. "Joking aside. Watch your step."

"I will. See you tonight."

Michelle went blithely through her day anticipating another evening with Tom. Her spirits were heightened by the sale of an expensive piece of property. In her buoyant mood she became careless and failed to notice the blond man whose car followed her to the late appointment.

    The maroon Ford continued down the street as Michelle turned into the parking lot of her apartment but stopped several blocks down. The blond man left the car and approached the apartment building on foot. He watched as Michelle greeted Tom and unlocked the door while Lucisi held the pizza box. To his disappointment Michelle did not go to her mailbox but sent the detective. After Lucisi had closed the door behind him the blond man sighed, retraced his steps to the car and drove away.

    Inside Tom thumbed through the mail. "No unmarked envelopes," he reported.

    "That's a relief. I hope you don't mind the change of menu. This has been a good day for me and I wasn't in the mood for chicken. Pizza seems more like a celebration. Surely an Italian can always eat pizza," she finished with a teasing grin.

    "This one can," Tom assured her. "And this one is also starving. Mike and I grabbed a hot dog about two and have been on the run all day. You'll be lucky if you get a second piece of pizza tonight."

    As they were finishing the food the phone rang. They exchanged looks and Michelle said, "Why don't you answer it?"

    "What if it's one of your boyfriends?"

    "Check the display box. If it's local I'll answer."

    A quick glance told them that a phone in

California was the source of the call.

Tom picked up the receiver. At the sound of his, "Hello," a click echoed in his ear as Clint immediately hung up.

"Well, he certainly didn't want to talk to me," commented Lucisi. "I wonder what he thinks about a man answering." The phone rang again. "That answers my question. He thinks he dialed the wrong number. Look. It's the same phone. He's never done that before, has he?"

"Not since I got the Caller ID. He changes phones for each call."

The ringing persisted.

"Shall I answer again?" asked Lucisi.

Michelle paused then nodded. "Please."

Once more Clint's response to a masculine voice was a click.

"Do you think he'll try another time?" asked Michelle.

"We'll find out soon enough. Let's retire to the living room."

Clint glared at the receiver as if it held the responsibility for his failure to reach Michelle. He walked slowly back to his car and sat without turning on the ignition. After a few minutes he began to drive, pondering this new development.

Who was the man who answered Michelle's phone? His identity had no relevance for Clint except as he shielded Michelle from Clint's calls and thus deprived him of the sound of her voice. He considered the possibility that she had contacted the police and rejected it. Police didn't sit by a person's phone. If they were involved she would answer and try to keep him talking long enough for a trace. The man who answered had to be a friend or relative. Maybe he would leave soon. Clint would call again later.

Tom sat on the sofa and watched Michelle sort through the day's mail.

"Anything that strikes you as unusual?" he inquired.

Michelle shook her head. "Same old, same old."

"Then come sit down beside me and tell me your life story." Lucisi patted the cushion next to him.

"That's subtle."

He offered her a dazzling smile. "Right to the point. Yes, sir, that's me."

She returned the smile and took the indicated seat.

"Seriously, you know about my job and that I like to cook and have met my aunt and my niece and nephew. All I know about you is that you work in real estate and someone or ones is making your life miserable. Oh, yes. You also like suspense movies.

"What else do you like? Have you lived here all your life? Where is your family? Would you like to go to a late show tomorrow night? There's a thriller on." He looked at her expectantly.

Michelle broke into laughter. "Okay, what do you want to know first?"

"Start with the most important. What about tomorrow night?"

"I'd like to go with you."

"Great! Now you choose the next topic."

"We'll begin with the hardest." A look of intense sadness crossed Michelle's face and she closed her eyes as if blotting out an unpleasant scene.

"I'm all that's left of my family. Just after I graduated from college I was offered a job here. I was raised in a little town in Missouri." Michelle continued tonelessly as if she were reciting information by rote. "Several years ago my parents and my younger brother and sister were driving to see me when an eighteen-wheeler slid on wet pavement and jackknifed into them. The car was completely crushed. It's not something I talk about very often." Her voice broke slightly. "Supposedly time heals all wounds but so far it's been a pretty ineffective medication."

Tom put his arm around her and pulled her gently against him. "I'm sorry, and sorry I asked."

"It's okay. I'm really too sensitive. It's just that I miss them so much." To her horror Michelle lost her normal, carefully guarded composure and burst into tears.

Lucisi held her closely and wisely said nothing, allowing her to release the emotional build-up brought on not only by the unhappy memories but also by the strain of being stalked.

After a few minutes Michelle lifted her head from his shoulder and said, "Forgive me. I'm so embarrassed. Usually I don't cry in front of anyone."

"Don't be sorry. I'm flattered to have you cry to me."

Tom's kind words soothed Michelle's shattered confidence and she once more sank back into his embrace. They sat quietly that way for some time then the detective glanced at his watch.

"It's late. I'd better be going."

"Not as late as the end of a late show." Michelle was reluctant to break the tranquility of the moment.

"Ah, but day after tomorrow I'm off. No early a.m. clock-punching."

Michelle sighed and Tom lifted her face to his. His lips touched hers lightly. He drew back and his eyes seemed to bore into the core of her being. He lowered his lips to hers once more then suddenly he was kissing her eyes, her cheeks, her nose, the corners of her mouth. She parted her lips and felt his tongue touching hers, exploring her senses and waking untouched feelings deep within her.

When they broke apart, breathing heavily, Tom whispered huskily, "If I don't leave now you'll need a whip and a chair to run me off."

Michelle sat forward on the sofa trying to catch her breath. "Neither one can be found here. I honestly don't want you to go but I think you'd better."

She stood and Lucisi pushed himself up to

stand beside her and take her in his arms once again.

This time Michelle took the initiative and gently disentangled herself from his embrace. "Please. We both have to work tomorrow and this is moving a little fast for me."

"Okay." Tom held tightly to her hand as he stepped to the door. "Be sure to lock up when I leave." He kissed her again softly. "Night."

CHAPTER 13

Michelle carefully secured the locks and retreated to her bedroom. Sultan, who had left his nook under the bed only long enough to glare balefully at Tom and grab a few bites of pizza, strolled out and regarded Michelle with a disinterested cat stare and jumped into her lap.

"You're going to have to learn to love him, Your Majesty," Michelle told him firmly. She stroked the Persian. "He may be THE one." Her fingers ran through the cat's soft fur.

When the phone rang she picked it up without thinking. "Hello."

"Michelle!" The voice on the other end of the line sounded relieved. "Where have you been?"

"What business is that of yours?" Michelle

demanded indignantly when she realized her California stalker was the caller.

"It's good to hear the sound of your voice," Clint responded in a caressing tone. "Sweet dreams." He hung up before Michelle could answer, leaving her sitting there, phone in hand.

If he had been the type Clint would have whistled cheerfully as he returned to his car and drove away from the phone. All the way to his apartment he smiled, congratulating himself on his persistence and his success in finally hearing Michelle's voice.

Upon reaching home he immediately began to write and sunrise found him bleary-eyed but well along on his screenplay. The phone contact with Michelle had been the impetus he needed to spur his creativity.

Pete, dropping by to check on his friend the next afternoon, discovered him still in bed, sound asleep. He shook him hard and then jumped back. Clint roused up flailing his arms and muttering incoherently. He swung his feet to the floor and sat on the side of the bed shaking his head.

Pete went to the kitchen and found a jar of instant coffee. Within minutes he was back beside Clint holding a steaming cup out to the director. Clint took the cup and sipped the hot liquid gingerly.

"What time are you supposed to see Raven?" Pete asked.

"That was last night," mumbled Clint. "I went

by for her but we promptly picked up right where we left off. I didn't stay long."

"Judging from the evidence in the other room I'd say she inspired you anyway. Did you work all night?"

"Uh-huh, but Raven wasn't the contributor. Michelle finally answered the phone."

"Michelle wh . . .? Oh, the woman you're harassing."

"Damn it, Pete! I wish to hell you'd stop using that term," Clint snapped, now fully awake. "It's more like a frigging practical joke. She's bound to have figured it out. She knows the calls are long distance. How the hell could I stalk her from miles away?" Clint glared at his friend.

"How do you know she knows they're long distance? What haven't you told me, Clint?" Pete returned the stare coldly.

"Shit! You didn't want to hear it. Remember?"

"Now I do."

"The bitch IDed the area code. Obviously she bought Caller ID."

"No wonder the woman wasn't picking up the phone. Who wants to talk to a nut? It's like inviting him in if you are aware who's there and answer anyway."

"Are you calling me a frigging nutcase? Terrific friend."

"If the shoe fits, Clint. Surely you don't think this obsessive phone campaign is normal."

"Shit, no. It's frigging unique. Not every woman can be blessed with the sound of my voice each day."

Pete regarded his friend with an disbelieving shake of his head. "Clint, *you* are too much. Whatever is going on with you, you'll be on your own as far as I'm concerned. My agent called this morning. Sunday I leave for Chicago to work on that TV movie I told you about. It's not the part I wanted but the character is sleazy enough to get me noticed even without a lot of air time. I'll be gone at least two weeks."

"Congratulations!" Clint reached over and shook his friend's hand. "I know how much you wanted this."

"Thanks. It's a break for me. I hate to admit I'm excited about it, but I am. Think you could manage to celebrate with me tonight?"

Clint grinned. "Sure. We'll paint the damn town red."

Michelle answered the buzz of her phone hoping it was business rather than the stalker.

"I forgot to tell you what time tonight," Tom greeted her.

"When does the show start?"

"Nine-ten or so. I'll be at your place around eight.

"Did you have any calls after I left?"

"Yes, and dumb me picked it up without thinking. It was the same voice from a California number. You know what, Tom?" Michelle didn't wait for an answer to her rhetorical question. "I would be willing to swear that he was relieved when he heard me. Like he had been missing me or something. Is that weird or what?"

"Not especially. If he didn't have some type of fixation on you he wouldn't keep calling."

"Thanks a bunch. I had begun to feel calmer about these calls since he's so far away. Now I feel creepy again."

Tom laughed without humor. "Don't start accepting the situation. You play right into his hands. Also remember that, no matter where the calls originate, someone here seems to be following you."

"Okay. Could we talk about this tonight? I have a call on another line."

"Sure. See you then."

In spite of Tom's warnings and her own uneasiness over a possible break-in (she had begun to wonder if she herself had displaced the jewelry - with the help of the cat), Michelle kept forgetting to watch for the stalker. She was bold by nature, used to doing what she pleased and going wherever she wished. The attacker-repellent she carried was as much to placate her friends as because she felt the need of it. Even before she was left alone by the loss of her family Michelle had firmly maintained her independence.

As a result she scarcely noticed the cars around her and would have been surprised and disconcerted if anyone had told her a battered maroon Ford followed her the entire time she ran errands before going home to scramble eggs and pop bread into the toaster for a quick supper. Afterwards Michelle showered and changed into casual clothes hoping that Tom's invitation to a late show indicated a lack of formality.

When Michelle opened the door for Lucisi she was gratified to see that he also had changed from work clothes to jeans and a knit pullover.

"Hi. Come on in and I'll get my purse."

"No hurry. We have plenty of time." Lucisi settled himself into a chair. "Tell me about the phone call. What did he say?"

"He asked me where I'd been, the same way Angie would if she'd been trying to reach me and couldn't. Then he told me he was glad to hear my voice. It was really strange, like a friend checking up on me."

"Don't give in to that attitude," Tom instructed her sternly. "If you do, he wins."

"Maybe I should get an answering machine. Do you think he might leave a message? I'd like for you to hear the way he sounds."

"Good idea. I'll pick up one for you tomorrow."

In spite of Tom's muttered comments concerning Hollywood's concept of police work Michelle enjoyed his company and the film. They arrived back at her apartment all too soon to suit her.

As they reached the door she asked, "Would you like to come in?"

"For a few minutes."

Sultan stalked across the floor to greet Michelle when they entered but neatly avoided Tom's outstretched hand.

"I don't think your cat likes me."

"Maybe that should tell me something," Michelle teased.

"Nah. It's dogs who sense undesirableness in people. Dogs love me."

Michelle looked at him skeptically.

"Promise," he assured her.

Sultan crawled under the coffee table out of Tom's reach.

"Why don't you check to see if you've had any calls?" the detective suggested.

Michelle agreed and Tom followed her into the bedroom.

"Not even a friend," Michelle reported.

"Maybe he's taking a night off."

"Could be. He's been calling between five and six this week. When I don't answer he keeps on until the early hours of the morning. It's as if he has a schedule."

"Perhaps he does. That might be a clue, if we ever get him pinned down. Realistically the L.A. police have too much to do to spend time on something like this. Anyway, someone calling from California doesn't worry me the way the man here does. Be sure to keep an eye open when you go out tomorrow. Remember, the weekend is when we've noticed him."

"I will. Tomorrow I'll be doing my regular

chores - laundry, grocery store and the like."

"And if he's established a pattern for you that's exactly what he'll expect."

"I guess so. That's not a cheerful thought."

"Do you want me to go with you?"

Michelle smiled up at him. "It's sweet of you to offer and I do appreciate it, but I refuse to allow some stranger to control my activities. I'll go alone and be careful."

"See that you are." Tom leaned down to kiss her and Michelle was intensely aware of the nearby bed.

She backed away and led him into the living room where he took her into his arms and kissed her compellingly. Michelle responded with passion of her own and they moved to the sofa as one being.

Later when Michelle was alone with Sultan she thoughtfully considered her relationship with Tom. She loved his gentleness and his willingness to move slowly. Michelle had done her share of fighting off persistent dates. Tom's easy acceptance of the limits she set impressed her. All it took was a word or a gesture. His indomitable self-confidence was not disturbed when she resisted a move. Tom didn't pressure or make demands. It was simple for her to relax in his company.

What perturbed Michelle about Tom was the fact that she enjoyed his company excessively. She doubted the concept of love-at-first sight and feared becoming too involved, too quickly. Since the death of her family she had rejected new relationships of any depth and shrunk from emotional involvements.

Of course, Michelle reminded herself, she might be taking too much for granted. Tom's attraction to her could be a passing fancy. His failure to press her further was possibly the result of a lack of interest.

Michelle shrugged mentally. Time would tell. As she wasn't anxious to establish serious ties, she could simply wait to discover Tom's intentions and cross that bridge when she reached it.

CHAPTER 14

The next morning Michelle was sorting laundry when Angie called.

"What's going on with you today?" Angie asked.

"Usual Saturday chores, nothing special. You have something in mind?"

"Yeah. It's not exciting, but how would you like to go mattress shopping with me?"

"Why? Your place is furnished."

"But I've been waking up every morning with a terrific backache and a new mattress is definitely in order. Please come with me."

"Okay, if we can also do my laundry. By the time you get here I'll have it sorted and be ready."

"Sure. See you later."

Michelle frowned as she restacked her dirty clothes. Where was the soft blue and white nightgown? She looked in the drawer. Not there either. A search of the closet determined that she had not inadvertently put it on a hanger. Michelle was standing in the middle of the room, hands on hips, scowling when the doorbell rang.

Angie entered and a glance at her caused a smile to replace Michelle's frown.

"I still can't get used to you as a redhead."

"Adjust. I like it. I'm about to decide redheads are the ones who have more fun."

Michelle laughed.

"Good. Now see if they can solve mysteries. I can't find my blue and white nightgown, the one that is such soft cotton. When I couldn't find it the other night I thought it was in the wash, but it's not with the dirty clothes either."

"When did you wear it last?"

"A week or two ago, I guess. That's not the kind of thing you write on your calendar."

"Okay, let Angie, the detective, take over the case. Say, you didn't by any chance leave it with Detective Adonis, did you?"

"No!" Michelle said forcefully. "I did not!"

"Don't be touchy. I was just kidding."

Angie rapidly went through drawers, closets, even the bathroom cabinet, but no blue and white gown was to be found.

"This is really strange." Michelle's face gave testimony to her uneasiness.

"Are you sure you didn't give it away?"

"Yes. That gown is one of my favorites. I know it was here. I didn't get rid of it."

"Well, it's not here now. Certainly no one would break in and only steal a nightgown."

Horror flickered in Michelle's eyes. "Only someone who was stalking a person. Angie, I'm frightened. It would take a real nut to want my nightgown."

Angie nodded sympathetically. "Yeah. Maybe you should stay with me for a few days."

"No! There must be a way to protect myself without running. If I let him intimidate me I'll never be able to look myself in the mirror again. Tom will be in contact sometime today. He should have some suggestions. After all, he is a trained policeman."

"Speaking of - how does the relationship with the handsome detective progress?"

"He's wonderful, too good to be true. I keep thinking I'll turn around and - Poof! - he'll be gone."

"That's great. It's about time you opened up to someone. You've been folded up within yourself since the accident. It's nice to be self-sufficient but, as your best friend, I'll tell you you've carried it too far sometimes."

Michelle withheld comment.

"Let's not worry about the gown right now," Angie suggested. "Get the rest of your clothes and we'll shop and do laundry."

The blond man watched as the women drove away. He waited several minutes before casually strolling to Michelle's door and letting himself into the apartment.

In Michelle's bedroom he opened the closet and reached in, choosing an item of clothing at random. It was a straight silk dress in a shade of soft turquoise, one that required dry cleaning. Michelle tried to get at least two wearings between cleaning bills and it held the faint scent of her perfume. The man brushed the dress against his face and breathed deeply, imprinting the fragrance into his senses. He held the garment in his arms and stroked it, then sighed and returned it to its place. Michelle would quickly miss that item.

Sultan watched from his hiding place under the bed as the man crossed to the dresser and began to open drawers. The intruder ran his hands over the clothing, careful not to leave disruptive evidence of his touch. His fingers caressed Michelle's bras and panties and he returned them reluctantly to their previous positions.

After closing the drawer the blond man checked his watch as he moved to the bathroom. Plenty of time before noon, the earliest Michelle and Angela came back on Saturdays.

The man eyed Michelle's make up but was cautious with his touch. The jars and tubes would hold fingerprints well, unlike clothing. His glance flickered over the array of cosmetics and on one shelf he noticed a new toothbrush. He reached for it, aware of everything he touched. He pulled Michelle's toothbrush from its holder and stuck it into his shirt pocket. Breaking open the package, he used a tissue to remove the new brush and put it in place of the old one. Then the man slipped Michelle's toothbrush into the packaging and thrust in under his shirt next to his body.

Before leaving the blond man made a hasty survey of the apartment and, certain he had left no tell-tale signs, let himself out. No one noticed him as he walked easily away from the building and down the street to the maroon Ford that waited for him.

Shopping for a mattress was more complicated than Angie had anticipated and they stopped for a burger before going to the laundromat.

It was after two when they returned to Michelle's and the message indicator on the call display box was blinking. Michelle hit the review button.

"I surely am popular today." She held the box for Angie to see. "Two calls from California (he's early today, must be taking advantage of weekend rates), one from Scott, and three from Tom. I'd better return his calls."

Angie chuckled. "Better? Does this mean he has the power over you?"

"No, but he worries. I forgot he said he was bringing an answering machine to hook up to my phone. Hope he called and didn't waste a trip over."

Michelle dialed Tom's number. "Fifth ring. Now he's not at . . . . Tom, it's Michelle. You rang?" she asked whimsically.

"Yeah. Are you okay?"

"Of course. Angie picked me up. We were running errands and time got away from us."

"Will you be home for a while? I'll bring the answering machine if you are."

"That'll be fine. We'll be here."

"If he's coming over now, I'll get out of the way," Angie said after Michelle hung up the phone. "Call me later."

"Angie! The idea! Stay. He won't be here long. I'd rather you didn't go."

"Are you sure?"

"Yes. I had thought maybe we go out or rent a movie tonight - unless you have something else planned."

"Actually Wes Davis wanted me to go out with him but he's such a bore. I told him I thought my college roommate was coming and he should check with me today. Then I arranged to be unavailable by phone. I'd just as soon stay in and watch movies. If we go out we'll be sure to run into him. Wes knows we didn't go to college together."

"That suits me."

The doorbell rang and Michelle let Tom in. He greeted them cheerfully and held out a box.

"My brother gave me this for Christmas several years ago but I soon got tired of people being able to make me feel guilty for not returning calls. Now they have to keep trying if they want to talk to me. It even has a tape with cute messages."

"Thanks. You want to attach it for me?"

"Sure." Lucisi took the now-familiar path to

the phone. In a short time he asked, "What type of message do you want on here? If you're going to make a straight one your voice should be the one your caller hears. If you prefer something cutesy pick one from this tape."

"I'll record a plain one, the leave-your-name-and-number type."

"Fine."

When the answering machine was set up Tom asked, "Did either of you notice any suspicious characters today?"

"I didn't," volunteered Angie.

Michelle shook her head. "Me neither."

"Are you going out tonight?"

"Just to pick up a couple of videos. Would you like to join us?" Michelle responded.

"Thanks, but no. There are some things I need to take care of. Do you have plans for tomorrow? If not, my sister Carla told me to ask if you'd have dinner with us, say about one."

Michelle hesitated. Angie nudged her with a go ahead look in her eyes.

"That would be nice - if you're sure she wants me."

"If she didn't want you she wouldn't ask you, believe me," Tom assured her. "I'll come by for you about twelve-thirty." He started for the door.

"Aren't you going to tell him about the gown?" Angie asked.

Michelle threw Angie a dark look and shook her head.

"What gown?" inquired Tom.

Michelle blushed. "It's too silly to mention. The gown will turn up."

"What gown?" Tom repeated.

"One of my nightgowns seems to be missing. I can't find it in my dresser and it wasn't in the wash."

"I searched, too," put in Angie. "It's not here."

"Was anything else missing or out of order?"

"Not a thing."

"I asked if she wanted to stay with me but she doesn't," Angie commented.

"What puzzles me is how someone is getting in." Frustration showed in Tom's voice. "Are you sure you don't want to stay some other place, Michelle?"

"Yes." Firmness was in both her face and tone. "I'll be careful and I'll be all right."

"Okay. See that you take every precaution and call if you need me. Otherwise I'll see you tomorrow."

After Lucisi left Michelle turned to Angie and said, "I can't believe you brought that up. Whatever possessed you?"

"He's a policeman. He needed to know."

"I was going to tell him later."

"Sure."

"I was. Anyway, what type of movie appeals to you tonight? Anything special?"

"Anything but Clint Sharkey. We'll both go to the video place. I don't trust your judgment and, anyway, I don't think your detective wants you out alone."

Michelle and Angie had no sooner left the apartment than the phone began to ring.

When he heard the answering machine click on Clint thought he had dialed the wrong number. Then he recognized Michelle's voice. He hung up and swore vehemently under his breath. Clint hated being pushed into difficult choices. He had no desire for Michelle to have a recording of his voice, but she might be using the machine to screen her calls and would never answer him directly again. Clint squealed tires to assuage his anger as he pulled out into the street.

From his vantage point in the hedge near Michelle's apartment the blond man monitored comings and goings. A brooding look settled in his eyes as he observed the detective's entry. This man appeared more and more regularly to be a companion to Michelle than any other male he had seen in the months he had been spying on her. If Lucisi was establishing a close relationship with the woman of his fantasies the blond man might have to act sooner than he had intended. He scowled. The man was a meticulous planner. Unforeseen changes annoyed him.

To his relief the detective did not remain long. Shortly after his departure the blond man watched Michelle and Angie leave. He debated following but decided to wait in his sheltered position. If they did not return soon he would go home and take up his surveillance again in the morning.

Michelle and Angie made the trip to the video store a short one and were back as it began to get dark. They were unaware of the man watching their every move. Habit motivated Michelle to pull the curtains as soon as they got inside and when the man could no longer see within the apartment, he slipped from his hiding place and made his way home.

"Are you sure you don't want to come stay with me?" Angie asked Michelle as she started to leave at the end of the evening.
"Yes. I am not going to be run out of my home."
"Okay. Call me if you need me. Or better yet, call Tom," Angie added with a sly grin.
"I'll do that."

When she was alone with Sultan Michelle played back the tape on the answering machine, which she and Angie had ignored through the evening. Scott had called again and there were three hang-ups that, according to the display box, came from California. Obviously her caller did not want to go on record.

Glancing at the clock she decided it was not too late to return Scott's call and he answered on the third ring.

"Scott, it's Chelle. I didn't wake you, did I?"

"Get serious. You know what a night owl I am. When did you get an answering machine?"

"Today. The police thought maybe my weird caller would leave a message but so far he hasn't."

"Is he still calling you?"

"Yes. So if Shawn Karlyn is back in the office he's certainly not my pest."

"He is."

"Did you want anything special?"

"No. I just wanted to check on you. I was hoping your stalker had gone away."

"Yeah, that would be nice."

After a few more minutes of superficial conversation they hung up and Michelle went to the bathroom to brush her teeth.

Sultan, who had been feeling neglected of late, wandered in with her and sat with his tail curled around his body. The Persian's eyes followed the movement of Michelle's hands as she picked up the toothpaste and reached for her brush. She suddenly paused and stared at the toothbrush with a puzzled look.

"Sultan, this toothbrush is green. I would've sworn my current one was blue."

The cat gazed at her as if he understood every word.

Michelle shuddered. She studied her face in

the mirror and spoke to her reflection. "I can't believe this is happening to me. It's unreal. Why would anyone do this to me?"

The girl in the mirror had no answer.

"Sultan, I am losing my mind." Michelle determinedly put paste on her toothbrush and began her nightly routine.

The phone started to ring just as Michelle sat on the bed and reached to turn out the light. She glanced at the display box. California again! In exasperation she snatched up the receiver.

"Do you have an accomplice here?" she demanded sharply.

Clint was taken aback by the aggressiveness in her voice and the lack of a greeting. Before he could pull himself together and respond Michelle repeated the question coldly.

"No," Clint replied mildly, still nonplussed by the fierceness of her tone.

Without another word Michelle dropped the receiver into its cradle breaking the connection and leaving Clint standing by the pay phone with confusion written all over his face.

CHAPTER 15

Michelle spent a restless night with multicolored toothbrushes dancing through her dreams when she slept at all. Finally around dawn she fell into a deep sleep and it was almost noon when she awakened.

Tom rang the doorbell while Michelle was still dressing. She threw on a robe and went to let him in.

"I'm sorry for not being ready," she apologized in answer to his quizzical glance, "but I had kind of a bad night. It won't take me but a few more minutes. Sit down and I'll be right with you." Michelle hurried back to the bathroom without waiting for his response.

"Was your harasser persistent?" Tom called to her from his seat on the sofa.

"He called once but that wasn't the problem," replied Michelle as she put the cap on her mascara and went to the bedroom to dress. "I don't want to shout back and forth. Let me tell you in the car."

"Fine." Lucisi thumbed through the Sunday paper while Michelle finished dressing.

When they were in the car on their way to Carla's Tom said, "Now, let's hear about last night."

"My toothbrush is the wrong color."

"What?!" Tom gave her a sideways glance.

"My toothbrush is the wrong color. I change my toothbrush fairly often. The one I was using was blue but the one in the holder last night was green. This morning it occurred to me to look, and the new one which should have been in its package on the shelf was gone. Somebody took my old one and replaced it with the one from the shelf."

"Are you sure you didn't do it yourself?"

"I even thought of that. The wrapper isn't in any of the wastebaskets and I didn't take out the trash between yesterday morning and last night. It shook me up badly." Michelle gave a rueful half-laugh. "You should've seen all the toothbrushes in my dreams. They would have been funny if . . . ." Her voice trailed off.

"If this were a laughing matter," Tom finished for her.

She nodded and said, "Yeah," very softly.

Lucisi was quiet for a moment then commented, "What keeps puzzling me is that there is no sign of forced entry. You didn't notice anything else out of order, did you?"

"No, but when I get home I'm going through that apartment with a fine-tooth comb. In spite of the missing gown the other clothing in that drawer was not disturbed. Nothing else was out of place in the bathroom. I feel like I've fallen into the 'Twilight Zone,' or maybe one of those 'Mission Impossible' plots where they completely changed the room to confuse someone."

"It's confusing all right. For this afternoon, though, try to put it out of your mind and enjoy my relatives. My family is special and I think you'll like them a lot. I hope so anyway."

"Okay. I won't mention my stalker."

Lucisi's family was all he had stated and more. Carla and her husband Tony were gracious hosts, giving Michelle the kind of casual welcome which said her presence was usual and desirable. She followed Carla into the kitchen.

"Is there anything I can do to help?"

Carla gave her the same merry smile that Michelle so often saw on Tom's face. "Just visit while I finish the gravy. Then you can help me get the food on the table. It's simple, quick-fix today, roast and vegetables." Her eyes twinkled. "I hope you weren't expecting something Italian and fancy like made-from-scratch ravioli or manicotti. It's not that I can't make them; I just don't make them very often."

"Actually I hadn't thought about it at all," Michelle assured her.

Carla stirred the flour and water mixture into the roaster. "How did you and Tom meet?"

Michelle paused, remembering that they had agreed not to talk about her problem. Still, Tom's sister was looking at her expectantly and she didn't want to be rude.

"I just walked into the police station and there he was. He could not have been nicer even though I wasn't exactly at my best."

Carla noted Michelle's trim figure and her big blue eyes in an oval face framed by shoulder-length soft brown hair. She knew her brother's weakness for attractive women and thus did not find it hard to believe that he had been at his most charming at their first meeting.

"Surely he wasn't arresting you."

"Oh, no!" Michelle exclaimed in a horrified tone, then realized that Carla was teasing her. "I had received a threatening letter."

Tom's sister raised an eyebrow. "Not really his specialty," she commented.

Michelle colored slightly, the flush in her cheeks making her even more attractive. "I discovered that the local police couldn't do anything about the mail, but the man who seems to be following me does fall under their jurisdiction."

Carla poured the gravy into a bowl and turned to stare at Michelle. "Someone is following you? How frightening!"

"Yes, it is. But Tom and I decided not to

discuss the matter today so I'd rather not talk about it if you don't mind."

"Sure. Here." Carla handed Michelle a bowl. "Please put this on one of the trivets on the table."

Michelle took the offered dish and went through the door into the dining room. Tom's sister followed with her hands full. She placed the casseroles on the table and said, "If you'll announce dinner to the rest of the family I'll get the rolls."

"Fine." Michelle stuck her head into the living room and intoned in a formal manner, "Dinner is served."

"Great!" Tony responded. "Come on, kids."

After the meal Michelle offered to help with the cleanup but Tom and Carla shooed her out of the kitchen.

"Go get to know Tony and the kids," Lucisi directed her. "I am now and always have been Carla's best scrub-boy."

Michelle obeyed and settled herself shyly in a chair in the living room. "They ran me off," she explained.

"They do that to me, too," Tony comforted her. "Carla and Tom have one of the closest sibling relationships I've ever seen. When we first married I was almost jealous but now it seems natural. Tom's a great brother-in-law - always there whenever any of us need him."

"That's nice."

"Take it from me, he's the kind of man you

can count on. I think of him as a true brother." Tony was interrupted by Teresa who held a small plastic doll in one hand and the doll's arm in the other.

"Daddy, please put Jenny back together again."

Her father took the toy and smiled at Michelle. "Time to put on my scrubs and become a surgeon."

Tony was giving Teresa the once-more-whole doll when Tom and Carla joined them. Their conversation centered on national and local events, including a charity event that was currently occupying a great deal of Carla's time.

During a lull in the talk Tom caught Michelle's eye and sent her a questioning glance. She replied with a slight nod and Tom said, "This has been an enjoyable afternoon but Michelle and I need to be leaving,"

"We've enjoyed having you," Carla responded. "Michelle, come back to see us. Our door is always open to you."

Good-byes were said all round and when Michelle and Tom were in the car he asked, "Did you have a good time with my family?"

"Yes, I did. Your sister has a knack for making people feel right at home."

"Agreed. I think she's pretty special. I'm glad you liked her. She liked you."

"Were you dissecting me while you cleaned up the kitchen?" Michelle inquired, half-angry, half-curious.

"Not really, but I did tell her about the stalker

and her thinking was in accord with mine. We think you should get out of your place until we determine how the intruder is getting in."

"No. How many times do I have to say that?"

Lucisi shrugged, unwilling to take up his half of an argument. "Okay. Just remember my advice is to go."

Quiet reigned in the vehicle.

Once inside the apartment Tom asked, "Before I go would you like to look around to see if anything has been disturbed?"

"I'll make a quick assessment but the things that turn up missing are so weird. It's hard to tell until I start some normal routine and discover something ordinary isn't where it should be."

Lucisi trailed at Michelle's heels as she scanned the apartment, stopping to check the display box, which was indicating phone activity by blinking. He noted two calls from California, from the same number, a rarity.

"Honestly, Tom. I can't decide whether or not anything has been moved. Nothing appears to be out of place. Still, after missing that gown, I'm just not sure anymore." Michelle plopped into one of the larger chairs by the sofa.

The detective did not sit but pulled Michelle back to her feet and put his arms around her. "Try not to worry. Sooner or later he'll slip up and we'll get a handle on him. The important thing, since you won't take a vacation, is to watch your step, or maybe I should say keep an eye out for whoever is watching your step."

"I will," Michelle started but Tom hushed her with a gentle, searching kiss. She answered with a sudden, growing passion and pressed her body against his, easing them toward the sofa.

Tom halted their movement and drew his lips from hers. "The temptation is almost too much, but I have to go." He reluctantly broke the embrace.

"Surely you can spare five minutes more." Michelle drew him to her one more time and felt Lucisi give in to his desire as his powerful arms pulled her even closer and he covered her mouth with his.

Later when Tom was leaving with his usual "lock up after me," Michelle reached up to him again for one last kiss. He resisted teasingly then kissed her deeply though briefly and walked to his car, turning back to see that she was locked in before he drove away.

The blond man felt an unbearable fury rise inside him as he observed Tom's affectionate parting from Michelle. The idea of any man but himself coming close to her was repugnant to him. All along his plan had been to find a way to casually cross her path and make her care for him with a passion such as the one he felt for her. Sensing Michelle's wariness of serious commitments, he had believed himself free of time constraints. Now he must find a way to separate her from Lucisi before they became more entangled.

The man's day had started early. He had found a secure place that gave him a clear view of Michelle's door without exposing himself to discovery. Discouragingly Michelle had not appeared at her door until close to noon and then only to pick up the paper.

Tom's arrival shortly thereafter had irritated him to the point that he changed his position in preparation for following should they leave. His efforts had been rewarded and when Lucisi's car had pulled from the parking lot the blond man had fallen in behind it at a discreet distance.

The man feared Tom. He knew the detective's reputation as a good and honest cop, tenacious as a bulldog on puzzling cases. If Lucisi observed the maroon Ford following his car the detective would certainly take steps to identify the owner of the Ford and the man could not take that chance.

Through more luck than skill the blond man had been able to keep up with Michelle and Tom and watched as Carla greeted them at the door. Deciding that the two would be occupied for some time, the stalker returned to Michelle's apartment.

When Sultan heard the key in the lock he crawled from his usual spot underneath the bed and strolled to the living room. One glance told him the entrant was not a friend and he scooted back to the safety of his hiding place.

The intruder shut the door behind him without concern for fingerprints. He congratulated himself for the forethought in obtaining surgical style rubber gloves. They allowed him much more freedom to handle Michelle's personal items.

Straight away he went to the bedroom and indulged his fantasies by stretching out on Michelle's bed. He turned down the covers and buried his face in her pillow.

The ringing of the phone startled him and he sprung up with his pulse racing. He stared at the phone and noticed the Caller ID readout. Closer examination showed him the California number.

While the phone continued to sound the man straightened the bed, plumping the pillow back into shape and carefully smoothing the bedspread. At last the ringing stopped but he was unnerved by the disruption and left soon afterward, taking only the spoon from the cereal bowl which remained in the sink after Michelle's hasty breakfast.

On his drive home the blond man pondered his next move. He needed to separate Michelle from Tom. Also his curiosity was aroused. Who could be calling Michelle from California?

Michelle felt restless after Tom left. She dialed Angie's number only to hear a busy signal. Sultan edged from his hideyhole and wandered into the living room. Seeing him, Michelle remembered that he had not had his evening meal and went to the kitchen. She absent-mindedly opened a can of cat food and dumped it into his bowl. He gulped the mixture hungrily. Michelle took his water bowl to the sink and filled it with fresh water. The Persian rubbed his head against her hand and purred as she leaned over to place the bowl on the floor. She scratched his ears and wandered back into the living room.

When Sultan had eaten his fill he strolled up to Michelle and pounced into her lap, knocking the magazine she was holding to the floor. He fixed his gaze on her face and cried, "Meow," plaintively.

"What do you want, Sultan? What are you trying to tell me, sweetie?" She lowered her face to his and the cat rubbed her nose with his own. Michelle brushed her cheek with his soft fur and the Persian cried again and nestled closer to her. She frowned. If only cats could talk. Something had surely disturbed Sultan during her absence. Of course the problem could be her absence itself, but a little voice inside told her it was more than that.

The sound of the phone interrupted her musing. She went to answer, noticing thankfully that Angie's number was the source of the call.

"Hey, Angie."

There was a pause before Angie said, "Oh, the Caller ID. It's spooky to have someone know you're there before they pick up the phone."

"I think it's great. You need one, too."

"That's okay. I'll just keep being surprised."

"Tell me. How was dinner with Tom's sister?"

"Fine. Carla and her husband and kids were all very nice to me. She and Tom are awfully close.

She backed him up on having me leave the apartment but I don't want to let this guy take over my life."

"Well, I happen to agree with them, Chelle. That man obviously has some way to enter your place without breaking in. What if he should come in while you're there?"

"When I'm here I put the chain and the deadbolt on."

"And if he doesn't use the door?"

Her comment was answered with a few moments of silence before Michelle answered. "That hadn't occurred to me."

"So now that it has will you come stay with me for a few days?"

"No. I still don't want to leave."

"Please, Chelle." Angie's voice was pleading. "I've got a bad feeling about this."

"Let's just change the subject, okay? What did you do today?"

"This and that. Nothing worth talking about. I called to find out if Detective Handsome's family was interesting."

"Would you please quit referring to him that way? His name is Tom. He *is* handsome but he's also very nice. Being with him gives me a warm feeling."

"I'm glad. And I'm kidding you when I call him names. Maybe there's a little jealousy involved, too. Every man I ever met who was that good-looking was a bore."

Michelle burst into laughter. "I'm so happy

that you called. Since Tom brought me home I have been feeling unsettled. You brightened me up."

"Is anything special bothering you? I mean besides the stalker."

"Sultan has been acting strangely this evening. He wants to cuddle up to me and is staying right by me. You know how independent he is usually. I can't figure out what the problem could be."

"Maybe the intruder was there this afternoon while you were gone. Did that happen to cross your mind?"

"Angie, don't even say that! Nothing is out of place. Tom had me check the apartment before he left."

"If you're sure you feel safe. I still think you ought to accept my hospitality."

"You're a good friend and I truly do appreciate the offer, but I'll stay here."

Their conversation turned to lighter subjects and when Michelle hung up thirty minutes later she felt more relaxed. She read through the evening and was starting for bed when the phone interrupted her.

In spite of the familiar long distance ID she picked up the receiver.

"Hello, Someone."

In California Clint took the phone from his ear and stared at it unbelievingly. He was taken aback by the lightness of Michelle's tone.

"Michelle?" he asked incredulously.

"Who else have you been harassing?" she

said sweetly.

Clint was speechless. The abrupt change in Michelle's attitude toward his calls bewildered him. He paused then matched her tone. "Only you, sweetheart."

Michelle giggled. "I've decided not to let your calls bother me so you might as well quit. Would you like to tell me good-bye for good now?"

As he was getting ready to engage in a bout of light-hearted banter a stab of fear shot through Clint. What if Michelle's willingness to talk was prompted by a police tap on her phone? Icy chills ran down his spine and he hung up quickly after saying, "Good-bye."

The director sat in his car breathing heavily, as if he had just finished running a marathon. He realized that his clothing was soaked with sweat. Pete's dire predictions played over and over in his head as he drove automatically toward his apartment.

Clint's first move upon reaching home was to reach for the phone to call Pete. Then he remembered Pete had left for Chicago that morning. He sat back in the chair and the clammy touch of his clothes against his skin suggested a shower.

The hot shower soothed Clint's mind as well as his body. He reminded himself that, even if his voice was recorded, a pay phone was the source of the call. His actions were surely not important enough to warrant the tracing of his voice pattern.

Thus he consoled himself, trying to relieve his anxiety by the assumed insignificance of his offense.

By the time Clint had toweled off and fixed a drink he was making fun of his earlier panic. He sat back in his chair and sipped the gin and tonic slowly. Soon the alcohol had relaxed him further and he began to test the next incident of his screenplay in his mind. Midnight found Clint engrossed in his writing, beginning another marathon work session.

Michelle hung up the phone feeling pleased with herself. Why on earth had it not occurred to her to handle the calls with a light touch earlier? She might have saved a lot of grief and worry for all of them. Of course the unseen intruder was a disturbing presence, but Michelle had become convinced that the blond man was not the man on the other end of the phone. If she could discourage her caller maybe she would leave the blond man for Tom to handle. She rolled over and was asleep before another thought crossed her mind.

CHAPTER 16

It was business as usual at Michelle's office Monday morning. She had begun to look forward to Mondays as Clint no longer called her at work and the blond man had never been in evidence on that day. Her co-workers had begun to joke about her Monday cheerfulness and wondered, for Michelle had confided in no one at her workplace except Judy.

It was mid-afternoon when Tom caught Michelle at her desk.

"All quiet last night?" he queried.

"California called again."

"I thought you had decided not to answer."

"Changed my mind. I tried something new though. When I saw the number I acted like it was a pleasure to hear from him. It obviously shocked him because he hung up in a hurry."

"Don't encourage him, Michelle."

"With luck that'll take the fun out of it for him and he'll quit. I wish I had tried this approach sooner." She broke off. "Here's a call on my other line, Tom. Can we talk later?"

"Yeah. Give me a call."

"Okay. Bye."

Michelle flipped casually through the mail as she walked to her door, glad to note that the threatening letters seemed to have stopped. Now if the mad California caller would stop she could focus on identifying the blond man.

Sultan met her at the door apparently having been resting in the large corner chair rather than hiding under the bed. She leaned down to scratch under his chin as she dropped the mail and her purse on the table. The cat immediately began to purr and rolled over onto his back. Michelle rubbed his stomach then turned back to lock the door.

The cat followed Michelle to the bedroom and watched as she changed from work clothes and checked the Caller ID.

"No one wanted to talk to us today, Sultan," she told him as he jumped up to curl beside her on the bed. Michelle dialed Lucisi's number and lay back across the bed absently stroking her pet. Tom answered on the third ring.

"Hi. It's Michelle."

"Any calls?"

"Not a one."

"How about blond men?"

"None of those either."

"I guess no news is good news."

"You forgot to ask about letters."

"Did you get another one?" Tom quickly grew serious.

"No, I just thought we'd cover all bases. Sorry."

"It's okay. We don't need a recurrence of that problem." The detective sounded relieved.

"I agree. Now if my caller decides he's not having fun anymore. . ."

"We'll have gotten rid of two out of three," Tom finished. "Still I wouldn't count out the phoneman. He's in the habit now. However Mike thinks you may have hit on something. If this harasser discovers he can't upset you, my partner believes he might stop."

"I hope so. Tom, could we come up with an idea to trap whoever is getting into my apartment? Somebody in California can't hurt me. Someone here is another matter."

"You're right. Did you uncover anything out of place after I left last night?"

"I didn't notice anything, but Sultan was acting really strange."

"Is that Sultan, the Invisible? How does he act when he's strange?"

"Clingy. Like he can't let me out of his sight."

"Are we talking about the same cat who won't

be bothered to greet us? That is strange. You don't want to hear this, I know, but I suspect someone was in that apartment while we were at Carla's - someone who unsettled Sultan."

"You're right. I don't want to hear that."

"You wouldn't take good, free advice and leave maybe?"

"You're right there, too. I know what free advice is worth."

"I'm beginning to know you pretty well."

Michelle was quiet, trying to decide whether to banter about the double meaning of Tom's comment.

Lucisi read her mind and jumped in with an uncharacteristic commitment. "And I'd like to know you better."

"Me, too," Michelle almost whispered.

Tom couldn't resist the opportunity to kid her. "You want to learn about yourself."

"No! You know what I meant!" Michelle's own sense of humor came to the fore.

"Dinner tomorrow night?" Tom invited.

"I'd love to."

"We'll be informal. Around seven all right?"

"Fine."

"See you then."

The next night Michelle spent extra time with her preparations, wanting to appear especially attractive no matter how casual the evening. When Tom arrived she met him with an affectionate hug.

Double Stalk

"Where are we going?"

"My place. I fixed one of my specialties for tonight."

"Great! It's fun to know such a good cook."

Michelle carefully locked up and they drove off.

The warmth of Michelle and Tom's greeting was not lost on the blond man. In spite of his fear of discovery the man had not been able to resist staking out Michelle's apartment after leaving his office. With rage boiling up inside him, he watched as Michelle and Tom got into the car and drove away.

Tom's duplex welcomed them with the fragrant odor of spices which filled the whole place. Michelle snifted appreciatively.

"Wow! Something smells wonderful."

"I put the meat in to season before coming to get you," Lucisi explained. He started for the kitchen and Michelle dropped her purse on a chair and followed.

She looked on, fascinated, as Tom wrapped a large dishtowel around his waist and began dexterously pulling ingredients from the well-provisioned cabinets.

He laughed when he caught a glimpse of the amazement in her eyes. "I've been doing this since I was a kid. Remember my Aunt Teresa?"

"Yeah. I just never knew a man who liked to cook."

Lucisi smiled and crossed the room to lift her face and brush her lips with his own. "Now you do."

Michelle rose from stool where she sat and put her arms around him. He pulled her into the warmth of his embrace and gently held her body against his, cradling her head on his chest, his face buried in her hair. Neither spoke, enjoying the closeness of the moment.

Finally Tom lifted his head and took a deep breath. "If we want to eat tonight I'd better get to work."

Michelle regretfully withdrew from his enfolding arms.

"I guess you're right."

Lucisi gave her a quick kiss and grinned slyly. "One of these nights we'll skip supper."

"That's a deal," she said boldly, then blushed.

The meal was both delicious and leisurely as Lucisi insisted that eating should be a social as well as a nourishing activity. Afterwards Michelle helped Tom clean up. As she shook out the dishtowel she glanced at her wristwatch and exclaimed, "Tom! Do you realize it's almost ten o'clock? I have an early meeting in the morning. I must get home soon."

"No problem. I'll run you back to your apartment now. And," he added with a twinkling smile, "I won't even come in and delay you."

"Thanks. Not everyone I know would be so

understanding."

After Michelle and Tom had said short good-byes, she locked the door and went to check the Caller ID, a procedure that was becoming a habit. Only one new call registered and, to her dismay, it came from California.

Michelle shook her head ruefully and commented to her pet, "Well, Sultan, that approach didn't work either. He's still calling."

The Persian stared at her with the know-it-all smugness characteristic of cats.

"At least you don't appear to have been disturbed tonight." She reached down to stroke his fur and Sultan arched his backed against her hand.

Michelle was still occupied with her cat when the phone rang. Another California number met her eyes. She sighed and picked up the receiver.

"Yes," she said in a bored tone.

"Aren't you glad to hear from me, Michelle?" Clint's familiar voice sounded in her ear.

"Not especially. I have a great deal to do and you are a pest."

"Aw, now. That's no way to talk. Don't be such a bitch, Michelle."

"Don't speak to me like that." Michelle calmly hung up and refused to answer the persistent ringing of Clint's return calls.

The following two nights Michelle had business appointments and was unable to see Tom, who voiced his displeasure about the situation and booked her next available night, Friday. She steadfastly denied Clint the satisfaction of hearing her by ignoring his calls. The blond man had not shown himself and by the time her date with Tom arrived Michelle had a feeling of normalcy. Had she known of the meticulous preparations being made by her fanatical admirer terror would have been her companion.

Lucisi followed the ringing of the doorbell with a three-two tap on the door. Michelle opened it and scurried back to finish getting dressed.

"Come in and sit down," she called over her shoulder. "I'm sorry to be late again but my last appointment ran late and you just can't rush a client. Use the time wisely. Try to make friends with Sultan. Here." Michelle dashed from the bedroom and dropped the cat into Tom's lap.

Cat and man looked at each other in surprise then Lucisi put a tentative hand on the nape of Sultan's neck and gently stroked the length of the Persian's body. Sultan arched his back in appreciation but only remained for a moment before jumping down and retreating to a place under the coffee table where he could scrutinize Tom judiciously.

The detective returned the animal's stare briefly then idly lifted the lid from the candy dish on the table.

"Hey! You need to restock your candy dish, Michelle. It's empty."

"I don't keep candy there, just the spare key."

Michelle emerged from the bedroom wearing a smile. "I'm ready at last. Shall we go?"

Observing the deadly serious look that had come over Tom's face she added, "What's wrong?"

"There's no key here." The detective's tone was even and businesslike. "When did you last have it?"

"I don't know. Several weeks or so." Consternation filled her eyes. "That's how he's been getting in, isn't it?"

"I would say so. He waited for the opportunity to come in when a workman was here and took the key when he left. Afterwards he used it to examine this place whenever he felt sure you would be away for a time. He's slick. I'll say that for him."

"I'll call Mr. Johnson. We'll have the lock changed."

"Yes, we will, but tomorrow morning would be the earliest time he could get a locksmith and Monday is more likely. I'm putting my foot down now, Michelle. You are not going to stay in this apartment until a new lock is on the door. When we finish dinner I'll wait while you pack a bag. You're going to Angie's or Carla's or even a motel - though I don't consider that as safe. He smiled thinly. My place is also an option but that might not be the safest place either. It's up to you where you go but go you will." Lucisi glanced down at Michelle's stubborn face. "Don't even think about arguing. I want you to go for your own safety, not because I want to order you around. I'm telling you this as a cop, not as your caring date."

The muscles in Michelle's jaws knotted as she pressed her lips together to restrain an angry retort. In her heart she knew Tom was right, but she hated being told what to do. The very fact that he insisted made her feel a need to resist.

"I'll call Angie," she said quietly.

"Do it from the restaurant. We will barely get there for our reservation as it is."

When Michelle and Tom had driven away the blond man noted the time. From their dressy attire he deduced they were going to be out for the evening and after peering about to see that no one observed his movements he casually unlocked the apartment door and silently entered.

CHAPTER 17

"This won't take long," Michelle commented as she inserted the key in the lock and stepped into her apartment.

Tom followed her into the bedroom. "Mind if we talk while you pack?"

"Whatever you want. I don't care," she responded coolly, still slightly miffed at Tom's demand that she leave.

"I wish you'd be more cooperative." Lucisi's tone was pleading though his words were not.

Michelle made no comment.

The detective was noting the ID display when the phone began to ring. "It's California," he told her.

"Here. Let me answer and you listen to the

conversation." Michelle crossed to the phone.

"Don't you ever give up?" she demanded.

"Michelle! I'm so glad you're home. You shouldn't neglect me the way you have."

"You shouldn't expect anything else. You won't even tell me your name."

"My name isn't important. Call me 'Someone' if you must have a title for me."

"I don't carry on conversations with people to whom I've not been introduced. Good-bye!"

"Wait, Michelle!"

She had started to slam down the receiver but hearing Clint's loud protest put the phone back to her ear.

"Why?"

"What would you do if we introduced ourselves?" he inquired gingerly.

Tom took the receiver from Michelle's hand. "I'd bust you so fast you wouldn't know what hit you," he snarled into the phone. "So quit harassing my girl."

Michelle snatched the phone back in time to hear a click at the other end of the line.

"Why did you do that?" she snapped. "He might have given us a clue to his identity. Did you listen to him at all? Whoever he is, my instinct tells me he's not dangerous and once I know who he is he might even stop calling."

"I'm sorry. You're right," Tom admitted shamefacedly. "It just made me so furious to hear him talking to you that my brain shut down for a minute."

"Anyway, what makes you think I'm 'your girl'?" Michelle challenged.

Lucisi turned her face up to his with a gentle hand and looked intensely into her eyes. "I say that because I want it to be true so badly. I want it now and forever. I love you, Michelle."

"You hardly know me."

"I know enough. This mystery has drawn us so closely together that I feel we've already known each other for a lifetime. I want you to marry me, to be my wife, and I've never felt that way about anyone else I've ever gone out with. Honest." His last word was spoken more in the tone of a little boy begging for belief than that of a man proposing marriage, but that one word and its tone won Michelle to reply in kind.

"I love you, too, Tom. At least I think I do. Since the wreck I've tried never to care deeply for anyone but I can't resist you."

She reached up and pulled his face down to hers and their lips met in a passionate kiss. Michelle felt Tom's hands running down her body drawing it closer to his. She melted into his embrace and together they fell to the bed. When they broke apart, breathing heavily, Michelle had lost all sense of time. "Enough, Tom. I'm not ready for this," she panted.

"I'm glad you said that. Being truly old-fashioned Italian I want my bride to be a virgin."

"I can handle that. How about you? Can you match it?"

"I'll take the Fifth," Tom conceded with a

chuckle. He shifted his position and leaned over to kiss her tenderly. "We'll let the past remain in the past."

"Are you sure I can't stay home tonight?" Michelle asked, changing the subject and breaking the mood. "I'll put the deadlock on so a key would be useless."

"No. Get your things and I'll follow you to Angie's." Lucisi pushed himself up and off the bed.

Michelle shrugged resignedly. "Okay."

Clint sat alone in his apartment and pondered his next move. Obviously he had misjudged the writer of the letter to the editor which had so angered him. First of all her voice was much younger than he had assumed. She also seemed to have a protective boyfriend who, from his threat, must be a cop. Of course the man could have meant he would physically bust Clint but the tone of the wording implied official action to the director. Third, this Michelle's variance of responses to his calls indicated more intelligence than Clint had expected.

He took a sip of his gin and tonic and lit another cigarette. Inhaling deeply Clint considered the idea of dropping the whole thing as Raven and Pete wanted. He shook his head and laughed at himself. No way. Too many years of living on the edge had made him oblivious to risk when something that gave him pleasure was at stake. No, he would not give up the sound of Michelle's voice, at least not before his current writing project was finished.

The fantasy of identifying himself to Michelle crossed his mind and he toyed with the whim but regretfully rejected it. The jealous boyfriend might make good his threat and Clint could not take a chance on that in spite of the flippant remarks he had thrown at Pete retorting to his friend's concern. Still the idea interested him. If his critic was also a fan the contact could travel down tantalizing paths. Clint licked his lips, almost drooling at the possibilities.

The director drained the last of his drink from the glass and went to the kitchen to make a refill. Tomorrow he would make another call. Perhaps Michelle would answer and be alone. Clint determined to keep trying. He was not finished with Michelle yet.

The blond man disentangled himself and crawled from his cramped hiding place in the back of Michelle's closet. He swore under his breath and wondered how long the object of his desire would stay away from her apartment. She had taken very little so maybe his best option would be to remain. Michelle could return in the morning, offering him the chance to carry out his carefully constructed plan.

Strolling into the kitchen the man contemplated a snack. If he had to spend the night waiting he might as well make himself comfortable. The intruder began opening cabinets to see what

Michelle's pantry held. Fortunately for him she kept an abundant supply of quick fix foods and he selected a package of macaroni and cheese.

The blond man was rinsing his dish when he heard a key turn in the lock and the voices of Michelle and Angie arguing as they entered. He rapidly thrust the plate out of sight and dashed back to his hiding place in the closet.

"There was no need for you to come with me," Michelle insisted heatedly.

"I can at least help you check for signs of a break-in," protested Angie.

"He doesn't have to break-in. He has a key."

"It's unbelievable that neither of us thought about that extra key. Think how many times I've used it to feed Sultan for you."

"Yeah. Look around. Not a thing out of place."

Angie walked into the bedroom and knelt to peer under the bed. "Nobody here but Sultan." She stretched her hand toward the cat who moved cautiously out into the room and blinked at the women. Angie scratched the cat's ears.

"It's a shame he can't talk," Michelle commented. "He could solve the whole mystery for us."

Angie nodded and asked, "Did you look in the shower?"

"Yes. I saw *Psycho*, too," her friend answered dryly. "You go on now. I'll be fine."

"All right, but I keep having a bad feeling about this."

Double Stalk

Michelle locked the door behind Angie and flopped into a chair with a sigh. "Sultan! Come here, kitty."

The cat came bounding in from the bedroom and leapt into Michelle's lap, snuggling tightly against her. She stroked him and breathed slowly trying to relax.

It had been a full day ending with a roller coaster ride for her emotions. Tom had completely swept her off her feet. She was totally enamored. Michelle daydreamed of life with the detective. She remembered the strong caress of his hands and smiled to herself as she reflected on his kitchen skills. Of course he could be rather domineering but most of the time he was consideration personified.

A sudden chill ran through her. The thought of making such an absolute commitment of her feelings was frightening. She had become accustomed to denying any chance for affection and shutting down rapidly any stirring of sentiment before it took the opportunity to grow within her. Even if she wanted to attempt to explain this to Lucisi, Michelle would never find the words to enable him to understand.

Floods of doubt swept over her. How could she overcome the self-inflicted crippling she had wreaked on her emotions and be a loving partner? Certainly Tom would believe he had made a mistake in caring for her when he became aware of her short-comings. A man from such a warmhearted family would undoubtedly expect more affection than she was capable of showing.

Michelle shook herself mentally. "You are being too hard on yourself," she scolded. Cuddling Sultan close she murmured, "You surely aren't deprived of attention, are you? If I can love a cat and care for you like I do surely I'm able to love a man who loves me. Right?"

Sultan gazed up at her, pushed himself closer to her body then yawned.

"If you're hinting that it's late, I can take the hint. Let's go to bed, Sultan."

Michelle had settled under the covers and was breathing softly and easily when the blond man crept from the closet holding a small paper bag. From it he took a bottle and a cloth and tiptoed to the bed. He stood there for a moment feasting his eyes on Michelle's sleeping figure. His stare was so riveting that Michelle stirred in her sleep, the intensity of his gaze piercing her slumber.

She roused slightly. The man's shadowy presence sank into her consciousness and Michelle bounded up only to be met by a powerful hand pressing a scented cloth against her face. She struggled but a few seconds before succumbing to the effective anesthetic.

CHAPTER 18

Angie ran to answer her phone. "Chelle? Are you okay?"

The voice she heard caused her to wince and curse herself for carelessness. "This is Tom Lucisi, Angie. Where is Michelle?"

"She insisted on going back to her apartment after you left last night."

Firmly restrained anger was clear in Lucisi's tone. "Why did you let her go?"

"Let her go?" Angie blurted. "You don't know Michelle. I stood between her and the door and pleaded with her to stay here. Nothing stops her when she wants anything badly enough. Sometimes she's too independent. She was so irritated with me that I couldn't even get her to promise to call me as soon as she got up this morning. I was hoping she had gotten over her mad and this call was from her."

"Okay," Tom said icily. "Hang up and I'll call her."

When she had broken the connection Angie muttered under her breath in disgust. She hated getting caught in the middle. Now both Michelle and Tom were aggravated and all she had done was try to be a friend.

Before Angie could throw off her vexation the phone rang once more. This time she only said, "Hello," noncommittally.

"Have you heard from Michelle?" It was Tom again.

"No."

"There was no answer when I called her. I'm going over there."

"Don't get excited. Remember with the Caller ID she knows who's calling. She's not happy with either of us. Chelle can be pretty stubborn. She could be ignoring your call."

"I'm going anyway."

"Tell you what. I'll meet you there."

"That's not necessary. The manager knows me."

"I'll meet you there." Angie hung up without waiting for Lucisi's response.

When the detective reached Michelle's apartment Angie was sitting in her car watching for him. She got out as he parked in the visitor slot next to hers.

"Hey," Angie greeted him. "I decided to let you be the one to disturb Chelle. Her car is right there so she must be sleeping in."

"I'd feel better if it were gone," Tom said tonelessly. He marched purposefully to the door, rang the bell twice and followed up with a strong knock.

Angie stood beside him listening but heard no sound of movement coming from within.

Lucisi rang the bell again and rapped on the door insistently. Still nothing stirred inside.

Tom turned abruptly away from the door and strode briskly toward the manager's apartment. Angie hustled to keep up with him.

The detective pounded on the door and called, "Mr. Johnson, it's Detective Lucisi. I need your help."

The manager swung the door open with a distressed look on his face. "What's the matter?"

Tom flashed his badge. "Do you remember me, sir?"

"Why, yes. You're the officer who was investigating Michelle Wilson's problem.

"Hello, Angie," he added, seeing her standing with Tom.

Angie nodded at him as Tom said, "That's right. This morning she's not answering her phone even though her car is out front. I want you to let us in to make sure she's all right."

"Of course, of course. Always willing to be of

service to the police." Mr. Johnson picked up his keys and scurried down the sidewalk.

"Let me enter first." Tom held out his hand for the key.

"Surely. You don't think anyone has harmed her, do you?" the manager inquired anxiously.

"I hope not," the detective replied grimly as he pushed the door open.

"Chelle," Angie called. "Are you okay?"

There was no answer.

With Lucisi in the lead they moved through the apartment. When they reached the bedroom Angie spoke.

"This is strange. At first glance nothing seems to be out of place. It's as if Michelle just walked out leaving everything, including her car."

"Where's the cat?" Tom wondered. He knelt and peered under the bed. Two glowing eyes glared at him. Cautiously stretching his arm toward the animal he called softly, "Here, kitty."

His efforts were rewarded with a growl and a hiss as the Persian spat and backed away from the probing fingers.

"I'll get him," Angie offered, pushing Lucisi to one side and kneeling by the edge of the bed. She wiggled her fingers tantalizingly trying to coax the cat into view.

"Come, Sultan. Good kitty."

The Persian remained stubbornly crouched out of reach.

After unsuccessfully attempting to entice the cat from his sheltered position Angie stood and brushed her hands on her pants.

"I have an idea," she said and started for the kitchen.

"Where are you going?" asked Tom.

"To find a can of tuna fish. Chelle usually keeps some on hand and Sultan can't resist it. That's his favorite special treat."

Lucisi and the manager heard the sound of cabinets opening then Angie gasped and ran back to the doorway.

"Come look at this. Michelle never left things this way."

Lucisi was moving before Angie had finished speaking, with the manager scuttling at his heels. Angie pointed to the dirty pan and plate hastily pushed among the canned goods.

"Don't touch anything. I'll put in a call and we'll check for fingerprints." He went to the phone.

Lucisi spoke for a few moments then returned to the kitchen. "They'll be here shortly. Let's wait in the living room. Try not to touch anything unnecessarily. We'll need to take your fingerprints to sort out the intruder's."

"Interesting," Angie remarked. "I've never had my fingerprints taken."

Tom smiled for the first time that morning. "Nothing to it."

Angie's answering grin was weak. An assortment of disturbing thoughts concerning her friend whirled through her mind.

The three of them sat without speaking until the team arrived. Lucisi rose to let them in then went with them to the kitchen to point out the out-of-place objects. He watched as they began work then went back to Angie and Mr. Johnson.

"This'll take a while. If either of you need to leave we can take your fingerprints now."

"I really have a busy morning," Mr. Johnson admitted apologetically.

"Not me. I'm here as long as you'll let me stay," Angie asserted firmly. "Anyway, sooner or later Sultan will have to be cared for."

"I can do it," Tom declared.

"Yeah, right. After all this activity has alarmed him even more," she snapped sharply. "He won't come to you now. You'll need my help with him."

"Fine. I wasn't trying to get rid of you."

"I didn't mean to overreact, but I'm awfully worried about Michelle."

"Justifiably. Me, too. I underestimated her obstinacy about leaving this place. I should have been more alert."

"It's not your fault. When Michelle makes up her mind a herd of horses running over her couldn't change it. I guess I could have stayed here with her."

"That would've only put you in danger, too."

"Then you really think she's been kidnapped?"

"I'm certain of it. In fact I had to say that to get the boys out here so quickly." Lucisi nodded toward the policemen working in the kitchen and bedroom. "An adult has the right to choose to be missing. Without a crime it would be forty-eight hours before an investigation would be started. We had to do something fast so I reported a kidnapping."

"You care about Chelle a lot, don't you?" Angie inquired boldly.

"As a matter of fact I asked her to marry me last night."

"Oh, Tom! That's terrific! Congratulations!" Angie paused. "She did say 'yes'?"

"More or less. She said she thought she loved me."

"Great! It's a good sign. I'm happy for both of you but especially Chelle. She's pent up her emotions for so long . . . she told you about her family?" Tom nodded. "Anytime a man got even close to her Chelle would find a million faults in him. I've been holding my breath hoping ever since she met you and she hasn't said anything about your faults yet. You'll have to be patient with her, Tom, but, as her best friend, I guarantee she'll be worth it. Before the wreck she was such a free spirit. If you can make her relax and enjoy doing things the way she once did I'll be your friend for life."

"You know how to be a good friend, Angie. I can tell. And I promise you I'll do everything I can to make Michelle happy." He hesitated. "The most important objective now is to find her. Do you think you might come down to the station later today and look at some mug shots? The man who was watching you two at the restaurant might have a record."

"Sure. I'll do anything I can to help get Chelle

back safe and unharmed."

When Tom and Angie were alone after all the furor they returned to the job of seducing Sultan from his hiding place. Angie stretched on the floor on her stomach and eased slowly under the bed cooing softly to the cat as she neared him. The Persian regarded her suspiciously. He had had his fill of intrusive humans and just as she reached out to touch him he leapt back away from her hands and directly into the grasp of the detective, who had moved to the other side of the bed in case that very thing should happen.

Sultan yowled in surprise and began to fight Lucisi's grip but Tom, by a lucky chance, had obtained a hold which allowed him to hang on while avoiding the cat's claws and he began to murmur comfortingly to the animal.

Gradually Sultan yielded to the inevitable. By the time Angie had wormed her way from under the bed and reached them the Persian was beginning to accept Tom's control. Angie stroked the cat lightly, marveling at the combination of strength and gentleness in the detective's hands.

After a moment Angie went to the kitchen. "Bring him in here and let's see if he will eat something." She emptied the abandoned can of tuna fish into Sultan's bowl and he attacked it hungrily.

"Poor baby," she said. "Chelle usually feeds him morning and night so last night early was probably his last feeding."

Double Stalk

"You're right. I noticed the remains of his meal when I came to pick up Michelle."

"He acts like he's starved although he couldn't be in such a short time.

They stood and silently watched the cat lick the final scraps of tuna from the dish.

"You know what, Tom? I believe Sultan might be better off staying at home. I can come by to give him food and water twice a day."

"I think you're right about leaving him here, but I'll take care of him. There's probably no danger for you but it would make me feel better to do it myself."

"Sultan isn't used to you."

"He'll have to get used to me. My problem now is deciding whether to have the lock changed or not. If the kidnapper came back he would be easier to trap inside than out. On the other hand I want Michelle to be protected as soon as she returns."

"Leave it," Angie suggested. "Michelle can stay at my place until the lock is changed. This time she should be willing to listen to reason."

"I hope so. Okay, I'll tell Mr. Johnson to leave the lock as it is and ask him for a key."

Tom and Angie had settled Sultan in and were at the door when the phone began to ring. They almost knocked each other winding rushing reach it. A California phone number was showing on the display.

"Answer it," Tom instructed leaning close in

order to hear the conversation.

"Hello," Angie breathed, still slightly winded from the dash for the phone.

"Michelle?" The voice on the other end of the line sounded puzzled. "Is that you?"

Angie glanced at Lucisi questioningly.

The detective nodded and mouthed, "Tell him 'yes'."

"Who else would it be?" she purred huskily.

"You don't sound like yourself." Clint's voice still held doubt. "What's wrong?"

"Just your persistent calls," Angie retorted briskly.

Her change of tone allowed Clint to differentiate between her voice and Michelle's and he snarled accusingly, "You're not Michelle! What have you done with her?"

Lucisi took the receiver. "The question is, what have you done with her?" he intoned menacingly.

At the sound of the detective's voice Clint panicked and slammed down the phone.

"He hung up again," Tom told Angie. "We might as well go."

"Why don't we dial the number right back?" Angie asked. "Maybe he'll answer. Stranger things have happened."

"Lucisi shrugged. "Go ahead."

Angie flashed the number up on the display box and dialed.

Clint stared at the ringing phone apprehensively, rapidly debating the pros and cons of answering. He feared the consequences of being identified by the man at Michelle's but was at the same time curious. Something odd was happening there and even over miles of phone lines Clint's feel for the dramatic could sense danger. Whatever was going on could have come straight from one of Clint's own stories and he wanted to be in on it. He picked up the phone gingerly.

"Yes." Clint tried to disguise his voice with a raspy whisper.

"Don't hang up," Angie commanded.

"Why?"

"Because Michelle didn't believe you meant her any harm and we need your help."

In spite of Clint's misgivings he was unable to resist asking, "Where is she?"

"We don't know. Do you?"

"Of course not. Don't be a stupid bitch."

Angie held her temper and bit back a sharp rejoinder.

"Are you taping this call?" Clint demanded.

"No tape. All we want to know is what, if anything, you know about Michelle's disappearance."

"I answered that. I don't hold conversations with stupid bitches. Good-bye."

"Don't hang up. Just tell me who you are."

Angie's appeal was too late. The line was dead.

Clint walked to his car shaking his head in perplexity. While driving home he mulled over the preceding conversation. Apparently the woman he had chosen to contact was in some kind of trouble. Rather than putting him off, the thought that she might provoke animosity or invite persecution only intrigued him. The director yearned to learn more about her and her present difficulty. The challenge was going about it in such a way that he would not endanger himself.

Clint wished for Pete. He desperately needed someone to use as a sounding board for his thoughts. Pete had not even left a number where he could be reached.

The director let himself into his apartment. He slouched moodily to the kitchen to fix a drink. Plopping into his favorite chair he lit a cigarette and began to picture scenarios concerning Michelle in his mind. Lighting one smoke from the butt of another Clint had worked his way through a quarter of the pack and was on his second gin and tonic when the phone sounded.

Without conscious thought he picked it up and was speaking before the idea occurred to him that his identity might have been traced. He stiffened, bracing himself to concoct a plausible lie, then breathed a sigh of relief as Pete's voice reached his ear.

"This must be mental telepathy," he told his friend. "I have been wishing for you."

Miles away Pete chuckled and retorted, "That has to mean you're in some kind of trouble again."

"Shit, no!" Clint's hair-trigger temper flared. "That's the frigging kind of comment you always make."

The director's ire did nothing to darken Pete's cheerfulness. "So. What's up?" he inquired. "I'm listening."

"It's Michelle," Clint responded.

"Michelle who?"

"Michelle, my critic."

"Ah, yes. Aren't you phrasing that poorly? Don't you mean Michelle, your target?" Pete ebullience over the success of his current role could not be squelched by Clint's bad humor.

"Something has happened to her."

"How do you know?" Pete swiftly became serious. "Clint, what have you done?"

"Damn! You're a fine friend. Nothing, you bastard."

"Okay. Calm down. Tell me about it."

"We've been talking a little bit. I seem to have imagined her all wrong. She stopped answering. Then her frigging boyfriend broke in on us once. Now today some strange bitch answered her phone and said they don't know where Michelle is."

"Has it occurred to you that this might be the way they've decided to stop your calls?"

Clint was silent for a moment then returned quietly, "No, it hadn't."

"Maybe it should."

"That's a hell of a thing for her to do - worrying me like that. What a bitch!"

Pete burst into uncontrollable laughter which only aggravated the director more. When he could finally talk, Pete broke into the string of obscenities pouring from his friend's mouth.

"Clint! You've been harassing her. You sent her threatening letters. You called and disturbed her at all hours. Why in the hell would she think you cared?"

"I hadn't looked at it from that viewpoint. Then you think I shouldn't be concerned?"

"Don't lose any sleep over it."

"Okay, but my gut feeling tells me that the bitch is in trouble."

"Forget it. There's nothing you could do anyway."

"Yeah, I guess you're right. How's the part going?"

"Great! This could be the big one for me. Maybe even move me from Pete Who? to major player."

"Terrific!"

"I just saw the time. I've got to run. Some of the cast are getting together in the bar in fifteen minutes. Talk to you later."

Clint was left sitting with the phone in his hand staring into space, still uncertain about what to do concerning Michelle. No matter what Pete suggested the director was convinced he had touched a bizarre situation.

CHAPTER 19

Michelle awoke wondering why her eyes wouldn't open properly. The realization that a blindfold held them closed caused a wave of terror to wash over her. She started to tear the cloth away and discovered that her hands were tied. New horror swept through her and she fought the desire to scream incessantly. An attempt to scream would have been useless anyway as she was also gagged.

She lay quietly, breathing deeply and trying to gather her thoughts. Her last clear memory was of getting into her own bed. What could've happened?

Vaguely she recalled the shadowy figure who stood over her like a nightmare. The dream must have been real. Now that it was too late she regretted her foolish stubbornness about remaining in her apartment. The blond man must have been hidden inside waiting for her. She had made it easy for him.

Michelle struggled to hold back pointless tears. Crying would do her no good and her strength of will made her determined not to show her fear to the kidnapper. All of her efforts needed to be focused on identifying him and escaping.

The sound of footsteps came to her ears. Michelle held herself still and tried to breath regularly hoping that he would believe she still slept. She could feel his eyes running over her body.

In spite of her efforts she could not restrain a telltale shudder, which cued the kidnapper to her consciousness. He sat beside her and stroked her arm lightly.

Michelle flinched away from the contact but was unable to evade the caressing fingers which played softly up and down her bare skin.

"Just relax, Michelle. I won't hurt you. You'll see. Before long you'll want my hands on you."

The desperate yearning in the voice caused Michelle to quiver with horror. Whoever had kidnapped her must be crazy. Only the firmest grip on her emotions kept her from whimpering with fright.

The man continued to glide his hand back and forth on her arm murmuring endearments. Fear tensed Michelle's muscles into knots and she forced herself to breathe steadily. Her captor stretched out on the bed next to her and pressed his body close.

She felt as if she were suffocating. He leaned over and brushed his mouth against her cheek. Repeating the movement he parted his lips and Michelle flinched as his tongue darted out to softly touch her flesh. He shifted his weight and passionately caressed her face, flicking his tongue along her cheeks, her forehead, her chin, every area which was not shielded by the blindfold or gag. No amount of mental concentration could prevent Michelle from blacking out from sheer terror.

She regained consciousness and had immediate awareness of the man lying beside her.

"I'm sorry, Michelle," he crooned. "I forgot to give you time to know me. I've wanted you so long." He broke off and buried his face against her stomach.

Michelle would have cried out if she could.

After a moment the man pushed himself up and stood by the bed where she lay helpless. He bent and ran his hands over her body giving special strokes to her breasts and thighs. Then he patted her on the stomach and turned to leave the room.

"Just don't continue to hold me off. I can't wait forever."

Michelle heard the sound of his steps exiting the room she occupied and sighed in relief for the respite.

Her mind whirled and she scolded herself severely. It was imperative that she manage to keep her wits about her if she were to escape this predicament. The harsh reality was that no one had the faintest idea as to the identity of her kidnapper.

It had to be Saturday by now. Surely Angie or Tom would discover her absence soon. She regretted the sharpness of her words to Angie, but best friends understood. Certainly Angie would call. Tom, on the other hand, thought she was with Angie and might not try to reach her until afternoon. Even then, what could he do? Michelle almost cried with frustration. Having been taken away unconscious she had had no chance to even attempt to leave a clue of any kind to help her friends locate her.

Sternly Michelle reminded herself that emotions wouldn't solve her problem. Thinking calmly was essential in order to make a plan to get away. And she refused to contemplate otherwise.

When the man returned later she could smell food. He sat down beside her and waved a plate over her nose.

"You must be hungry, Michelle," he said gently. "It's been quite a while since you had anything to eat. If you promise not to cry out I'll uncover your mouth and feed you. Will you do that?"

Michelle nodded and her captor put the food aside and removed her gag. He released the heavy strips of cloth across her waist and ankles which had held her body tightly against the bed and pulled her to a sitting position, propping her up with pillows.

Her mouth was stiff and Michelle wiggled the muscles to loosen them. As flexibility returned to her lower face she asked, "Who are you? Why have you done this?"

"I adore you, Michelle. I desire you. I worship the way you walk and move and smell. Once you know me, you'll want me, too. Trust me."

He covered her mouth with his and thrust his tongue into hers. His kiss was deep and prolonged. When he withdrew Michelle felt a strong desire to retch but hid her repugnance by masking her face with indifference.

The kidnapper drew back and studied her countenance.

"You can't fool me, darling. I know you really liked that. Relax and let me have your true response." He grasped her chin firmly and bent to her lips again.

Michelle steeled herself to endure the unwanted contact and was relieved when he finally rose and the odor of food told her that eating was next on his agenda.

He fed her awkwardly, pausing often to wipe her chin as he spilled the chicken mixture again and again. Michelle could only guess at the identity of the food, but supposed from the flavor and texture it was some sort of ready-made pot pie. In spite of the circumstances she found that she was hungry and ate eagerly.

"Could I have something to drink?" she asked.

"Of course, darling. What would you like?"

Michelle repressed a shudder at the sound of the endearment and inquired, "What have you got?"

"Everything that you usually keep in your apartment."

"Iced tea?"

"I'll get some." The man started to go but turned back to retighten the loosened bounds that had pinned Michelle down. "We wouldn't want you to hurt yourself trying to get up, would we?" He kissed her lightly on the forehead and she heard him leave the room.

Despair began to creep through Michelle. The stalker was so thorough and methodical. He had to have been planning this abduction for quite a while. He must have studied her activities for weeks, easily predating the letters and the calls from California. Now she was quite sure that the man who called her from California was not the man who held her captive.

Michelle almost laughed at the irony. Actually the caller might have done her a favor. Without his overt threats none of them would have suspected anything until she disappeared. At least now her friends would know that she was in trouble and would start looking for her immediately.

She listened carefully, trying to gain any hints of where she was. The kidnapper had allowed himself plenty of time to move her. It had been barely after midnight when she went to bed and it was surely Saturday evening, close to eighteen hours since he took her away. That length of time was sufficient to go across several state lines.

Michelle almost instinctively rejected the idea without conscious thought. Some inner voice told her that her captor would find a place closer to home, probably only a few hours away. The shorter the drive, the less chance there would be of anyone noticing her tied up in his vehicle. She wondered if she had ridden in the maroon Ford Tom had spotted or if this man was the same one who drove it.

Her musings were interrupted by the return of her would-be lover with a glass of tea. "Here you are. Just as you like it - one spoon of sugar, no lemon."

"How do you know that?"

"I've been watching you, Michelle. I know all about you, Michelle. Your name is very beautiful, like you. I love to say it over and over. Michelle. Michelle." He sat and held the glass to her lips.

She took a generous swallow. "Thank you. You know my name. What name should I call you?"

"'Sweetheart' would be good."

"Don't you have a name? You like mine. I might like yours."

"You'll find out soon enough. Would you like another sip?"

"Please." Michelle drank slowly as she tried to think of another tack to help her learn his identity.

"These pieces of cloth you've used to tie me down are really uncomfortable. Could you loosen them or take them off?"

"That will happen soon enough, too."

Something in his tone implied engaging in activity Michelle feared would be unpleasant to her and she refrained from pursuance of that topic.

"Have I met you before?"

"Don't concern yourself with the past. We have the entire future ahead of us."

Michelle cringed inwardly and decided no line of questioning was safe. Neither spoke for several minutes while the kidnapper gave her sips of tea. She finished the liquid and felt his weight lift as the man stood up and took the glass and plate from the room.

Hearing him leave, Michelle tested the strength of her bonds. Her captor had used strips of cloth for all of her restraints and the width of the material assured that loosening them would be difficult at best. Tearing them was not feasible either. She needed something sharp to start the cloth raveling. Maybe the next time the man fed her he would leave the glass.

It seemed that she had been lying there for hours when Michelle heard her captor re-enter the room. Without speaking he released the cloths which held her down and slid her over. Michelle held her breath. Had he decided to let her up? Her hopes were dashed when she felt the pressure as he tightened the strips again and lay down beside her. He rolled on his side, putting his arm across her and molding his body securely against her own.

Michelle felt as if she were smothering and futilely strained to pull away from his touch. His powerful arm controlled her as effectively as a straitjacket. She could not repress a whimper deep within her as he clamped down firmly and covered her throat with wet kisses. Her body heaved with silent sobbing and the man lifted his face and pulled back, propping himself on one elbow to stare at Michelle.

He ran a hand down her cheek. "Don't cry,

Michelle. I love you. We won't rush tonight. We'll just sleep here together. Tomorrow you'll want me more."

The words which her abductor intended as comfort did nothing to ease Michelle's anxiety but she forced herself to hold back the tears. She feared that out-and-out rejection might trigger violence in her captor. As her breathing became more normal he put his arm more lightly across her and nestled against her side. After a while she realized that he had gone to sleep.

Ann Snuggs

CHAPTER 20

Sunday morning Tom picked up the paper and let himself into Michelle's apartment then whistled before remembering that it was customary to call cats, not whistle for them.

Unconventional or not Sultan seemed to understand the significance of Tom's signal because he padded into the living room stretching and meowing questioningly as if to say, "What are you doing here and where is Michelle?"

Lucisi scooped up the cat and scratched him behind his ears. Sultan demonstrated his appreciation with a loud purr.

Carrying the Persian, Tom walked through the apartment slowly, his eyes scanning the area for any clue to shed light on the facts of Michelle's disappearance. Remembering the difficulty Michelle had in determining missing items he didn't actually expect to find one. The intruder was an expert at covering his tracks. Nevertheless, he looked. It would not do to overlook something because of carelessness.

It occurred to him to wonder if the kidnapper's planning had included taking any of Michelle's clothes. He thumbed through the closet but his knowledge of her wardrobe was too vague. Angie would know. He went to the phone.

"Angie, this is Tom Lucisi. I need your help."

"Sure, Tom. What can I do?"

"I'm at Michelle's apartment hunting for anything that might be out of order and just haven't been here enough to be certain. I'd particularly like to know about her clothes."

"It will be around forty-five minutes before I can get there."

"That's okay. I'll work on getting Sultan to accept me."

When Angie arrived she found Tom in the living room reading the paper with the cat curled in his lap purring contentedly.

"Why are you sitting here with the door standing open?" she asked.

"I'm keeping an eye out in case a maroon Ford should cruise through the parking lot."

"You don't really think he'll come back, do you?"

Lucisi gave a stereotypically Italian shrug. "Who knows? I just don't want to miss any bets."

Angie gestured at Sultan. "I see he's decided to permit you to hang around, although it's hard to tell who's in charge."

Tom chuckled. "Probably the cat. I can't say I invited him to interfere with my reading."

He stood up and Angie noticed with approval that, rather than dumping Sultan in the floor, the detective cradled him in his arms. As they moved toward Michelle's bedroom the cat squirmed and Tom lowered him gently to the floor. The Persian sauntered after them and sat in the doorway, his eyes fixed upon their movements.

"Can you tell if anything is missing?" asked Lucisi, opening the closet and indicating the clothing hanging in it.

"I'm not sure but let me take a look." Angie began to shuffle through Michelle's wardrobe. She examined the hanging clothes then started on the shelves she and Michelle had built into one side.

"So far everything seems to be here." Angie squatted and looked at the neatly placed items on the floor. "Wait a minute. These shoes are piled on top of each other. Michelle doesn't leave things messy like that." Angie wiggled toward the back corner of the closet. "This must be where the man hid, Tom. There's almost a nest behind these shoes."

"Let me see." Lucisi motioned for Angie to move aside and got down on his knees to inspect the area.

"Whoa! What's this? Hand me a tissue or something, Angie. I believe this may have fallen from the kidnapper's pocket."

Angie quickly snatched a tissue from the box by Michelle's bed and thrust it at Tom, who carefully picked up the item, backed from the closet and held it out for her to see.

"Is this Michelle's?"

"No." Angie stared at the pearl-handled penknife and reinforced her negative word with a shake of her head. "Michelle's not much of a knife person. Kitchen knives, sure, but I doubt that she ever owned a pocket knife, even a small one like that."

"Terrific! This is the first real concrete clue we've had. If they can get prints from it we might find a match. Of course, the perpetrator would have to have been printed at some time. However, right now I'll take any help we can get."

"Yeah. Me, too."

A further search uncovered no other irregularities in the apartment and by noon both Angie and Tom felt that they had exhausted the possibilities.

"Do you want to grab a sandwich or burger somewhere?" Lucisi invited.

"Thanks, but I really need to get home. My job is demanding and during the week my place has to take care of itself. I'm not organized like Michelle so there's always too much for me to do on weekends."

"Okay. I have things to do, too. I'll come back by here this evening and feed Sultan his supper."

"Good. Please give me a call if you hear

Double Stalk

anything." Angie turned to leave.
"I will."

Ann Snuggs

CHAPTER 21

Michelle's first conscious thought Sunday morning was one of amazement that she had been able to sleep at all. To her relief she was alone in the bed. The noises of the man stirring in the adjoining room came to her ears as she tested her bonds. They were securely tied, giving very little to her efforts to move them.

She dreaded the day and the company of her warped admirer. The man definitely adored her in his twisted way and seemed to genuinely believe that she would reciprocate his affection if he kept her close to him. Michelle shuddered at the memory of his touch then shook herself mentally. This line of thought was senseless, not to mention disheartening. A plan was necessary.

From the sounds and smells coming from the other room Michelle surmised that her captor was cooking, or at least heating food. She heard him swear and the clatter of a breaking dish told her that he had probably burned himself. Good, she thought savagely. Serves him right for doing this to me.

Michelle tried to block out the noises and focus on her strategy. Overtly defying him was out. Such a move most certainly would provoke him to force himself on her and possibly bring her severe injury. If she could stomach the necessary actions to con him he would be only too willing to believe that she was attracted to him. Her performance had to be convincing, not overblown enough to rouse any suspicions concerning her sincerity nor transparent enough to anger him.

If only she could see! The blindfold disturbed her more than the cloths that restrained her. At least he had not replaced the gag and Michelle intended to do nothing that might cause him to do so.

In spite of the anxiety her previous attempts at conversation had brought about Michelle decided that her best approach would be to talk with him. Perhaps she could ease his cautiousness to the point that he would release her bonds or, at the least, loosen then. Bracing herself for the ordeal ahead Michelle considered possible ways to open communication with her captor.

The odor of burned toast preceded the sound of footsteps as her would-be lover entered the room and asked tenderly, "Did you sleep well, darling?"

Steeling herself to endure whatever followed,

she responded, "Not very. And you?"

"It was a wonderful night for me, being so close to you after waiting so long." Michelle heard the plate making contact with the bedside stand and felt the bed give as the kidnapper sat down and leaned over to kiss her.

"Good morning, dearest."

Michelle winced and jerked away. "Oh! Don't kiss my morning breath! Please, let me brush my teeth."

The man stroked her cheek. "Your breath would always be sweet to me, darling, but, if you promise not to run away, I'll untie you so that you can brush your teeth and wash your face."

"That would be nice."

"Don't you want me to feed you breakfast first?"

"Can't I eat after you untie me?"

"No. Eat while it's hot."

Michelle gave a slight disapproving shrug. "Okay. Whatever you want."

Her kidnapper practically purred. "Those are the kinds of words I want to hear you say." He kissed her again and loosened the straps holding Michelle down just enough to pull her to a sitting position.

Plans to the contrary, she could not suppress the chill that ran through her in response to his touch, but she quickly excused it with the comment, "Oh! You're tickling me."

For some reason the remark seemed to please him and he laughed with pleasure. "I'll do more for you than that later," he promised.

Michelle's imagination conjured up horrible visions but she forced a small smile and said nothing.

The breakfast was atrocious, burned toast and overdone eggs, but Michelle forced herself to eat, thinking that she would need her strength.

Afterwards, true to his word, her abductor began to release her, taking every opportunity to caress her body as he worked. She reached for the blindfold but he grabbed her hands and held them down.

"No. Wait until I leave the room. It's better that you don't see my face yet. After I've locked you in you can remove it. You'll see that the bath is ready for you, even your toothbrush is there along with your brand of toothpaste. I planned everything to welcome you. When you have finished, cover your eyes again and call me."

"What if I don't cover my eyes before I call."

"I've planned for that possibility. If you want to find out how, do it." There was sudden menace in his tone.

Michelle allowed him to see her wilt at the implied threat. "Very well, I'll follow your instructions."

"Call me when you finish. I'm going now."

Michelle heard the door close and the sound of a key turning in the lock. She tugged at her blindfold and breathed a sigh of relief when she could finally tear it from her face. Rebelliously she flung it across the room and blinked at the sudden return of light in her eyes. She sat on the edge of the bed giving herself time to regain the equilibrium lost from the day of blindness and restraint.

Glancing around her prison she studied every detail trying to fix it in her mind for later identification. Michelle refused to accept the idea that she might not escape and the more clearly she described the place where she was held the more credible the story of her ordeal would be.

The room in itself was small yet pleasant enough. The walls were painted a pale yellow and the one window was curtained with ivory sheers on each side of the shade. Michelle staggered to the window and saw that the shade was tacked to the sill, undoubtedly to prevent her looking out. No pictures graced the walls and the furniture was serviceable but plain, the kind easily obtainable in any inexpensive outlet. The bed she had slept on was a double and filled most of the room. A small table stood beside it and a dresser and chair completed the furnishings.

The bathroom jutted out into the bedroom, obviously added after the original construction. As her balance returned to normal Michelle walked to the door and peered in. It gave her a creepy feeling to see the blue toothbrush she had only recently missed resting beside her usual brand of toothpaste on the lavatory and her heart skipping a beat at the sight of her own blue and white nightgown hanging from a hook on the wall. She took a deep breath and went in, shutting the door tightly behind her.

To her dismay Michelle discovered that the

lock had been removed from the bathroom door permitting her captor to enter at will and allowing her no assurance of privacy. Anger flooded through her. How dare anyone treat her in this manner! When she finally got out of here she would spend whatever time and effort necessary to see that this creep was punished.

Michelle stepped out into the larger room. Perhaps she could find a way to block the door. Even if it were only something to give her extra warning time, that would be better than nothing. Her eyes flicked over the minimal furniture. The bedside table. If she placed it against the door to the bedroom the man could not enter without knocking it over. The noise should permit her time to prepare for his entrance to the bathroom several steps away.

As quietly as she could Michelle tested the weight of the table. Dragging it would certainly tip off her captor, but if she could lift it . . . . Fortunately it was not too heavy and Michelle eased it in front of the door.

Michelle hurried in the shower but took her time brushing her teeth and fussing with her hair. Regretfully she passed up the clean gown hanging in the bath and put on the pajamas she had worn to bed the night she was kidnapped. They weren't exactly fresh but they offered more coverage of her body. Already she had had reason to be grateful that she had worn pajamas to bed that night.

"Michelle." Her captor was calling through the door. "You're taking a long time. Answer me so I'll know you're there."

"I'm here," Michelle called immediately. "The shower felt so good. I just stood there and relaxed under the spray. Just a few more minutes and I'll be finished."

"All right. Don't keep me waiting too long."

Michelle hurried to the dresser and rapidly checked the drawers for any item that might aid her escape. To her disappointment all the drawers were empty. They held not even a scrap of paper. The same was true of the drawer in the table. As silently as possible Michelle moved the table back to its original position. She sat on the bed wondering how long she could stall her abductor.

"Michelle." His voice was becoming more insistent.

"If you're in that big of a hurry, come in," she yelled.

"Are your eyes covered?"

"Not yet."

Michelle wished for some way to learn the time. She knew it must be Sunday by now, but her drugged sleep when she was kidnapped followed by the disturbed night combined with the lack of opening to the outside world had totally disoriented her. Maybe she could convince the man that more sleep was necessary and he would leave her alone for a while longer.

"Michelle!" Now anger could be detected.

"Just a minute."

"No. I'm coming in."

"My eyes aren't covered."

"I don't care."

The door was slammed open and Michelle swallowed a scream when she saw the face before her. Then hysterical laughter bubbled up. Her captor had shielded his identity with the head from an ape costume. "How fitting," she thought. He was an animal.

The first words from his mouth were menacing. "I see I can't trust you."

Michelle reined in hard to control her hysteria. "I told you I wasn't ready. You didn't give me enough time."

"I'm being very patient with you, Michelle." The stern voice contrasted sharply with the face of an ape. "It's unkind of you to take advantage of my thoughtfulness. You haven't even changed into the gown I brought for you."

Michelle wanted to scream at him that thoughtful people did not kidnap women from their beds but she bit her tongue and attempted to placate him.

"I thought I'd save it for later."

The hooded man sat beside her on the bed and reached for the cloths he had used to confine her.

"No. Please, no," she whispered, trying to keep her true fear and loathing from reflecting in her tone.

"I'm afraid so, darling, for a few more days at least."

Michelle fought the impulse to claw at him as he grasped her wrists firmly and bound them together behind her then placed the blindfold across her eyes. Her submissiveness gained her a looser bondage and temporary freedom for her ankles. She reasoned that, with her hands at her back he did not plan to pin her to the bed. Surreptitiously she tested the binding cloths and discovered a small amount of play. Now, if he would just leave her alone. . . .

Those hopes were dashed as he put an arm around her shoulders and asked, "Would you like to sit with me for a while. I have some work to do."

Michelle nodded docilely. "Why not?"

Her captor stood and pulled her to her feet. Guiding her with a touch that was uncomfortably familiar, he walked her into another room and seated her on a sofa. She settled herself awkwardly trying to adjust for her bound hands.

"It's hard to sit comfortably with my hands in the way," Michelle protested. "Why don't you tie them in front?"

The man sat beside her and drew her close to him. Michelle had no way to push him back as he kissed her passionately then nuzzled her throat.

"Because they would be in my way, dearest." He resumed his caresses. Michelle remained unresponsive, forcing her mind to block out the repugnant feel of his mouth on her flesh.

With sudden resoluteness he tore himself away from her and rasped huskily, "You'll have to come later. I have to complete this brief before morning." He stroked her cheek. "Anticipation will make it that much sweeter."

Her immediate fear alleviated, Michelle sighed

and breathed, "I can wait," hoping her sarcasm was not obvious.

The man rose and she tried to find a comfortable position. Soon he was back beside her. Michelle listened carefully and realized from the sounds that her abductor was shuffling papers and using a laptop computer.

Michelle's mind reeled. What kind of man was this stalker? Some kind of screwball writer? A frustrated professional man compensating for lack of recognition? A computer whiz hunting human contact? His skill in using the laptop was obvious. She could tell by the steady pace of his work.

A memory flashed into her consciousness. What had he said as he released her? He had to finish a brief. A brief! Her captor was a lawyer! Or maybe a paralegal. Whatever, it was a big step toward learning his identity.

It also came close to assuring Michelle that he would leave her alone to go to work on Monday. She must be very cooperative until then. She needed every possible concession to improve her chances of getting away during his absence. If pretending to succumb to his overtures would make him lax in securing her restraints, the likelihood of escape would be greater. Michelle would do whatever necessary to achieve freedom - preferably intact.

CHAPTER 22

Clint swore as he slammed down the receiver. This was the fourth call and the fourth pay phone he had used on the warm California afternoon to no avail. Michelle was refusing to answer again.

Of course, the bitch who had answered her phone yesterday could have been telling the truth. Nah, Clint threw out the thought. It was too absurd to think that Michelle had been kidnapped. What a great, thought-provoking screenplay that would make - a woman preyed upon by two stalkers. Actually Clint refused to define his behavior as stalking; he was simply aggravating a critic and, since he regarded critics as less than human, saw no wrongdoing in his actions.

Two stalkers! Both could be depraved and the

conflict would end in an explosive clash with enough panchromatic blood to do Peckinpah proud!

Clint almost ran to his car. He broke all speed limits going home and dashed up the stairs to his apartment. Resisting the urge to sweep the current writing to the floor in a heap, he stacked the pages neatly to one side, placed a new carton of cigarettes in easy reach, rifled through his notebooks for a fresh one and dropped to his working position by the table, a handful of writing utensils handy.

Within an hour his synopsis was complete and Clint had begun work on the rough outline of the screenplay. Never had he been so inspired. Stopping only for liquid and bathroom breaks he wrote as if trying to break speed records. The Muse which possessed him pushed him past his limits and eighteen hours later he roused and blinked his eyes becoming aware that he had gone to sleep - passed out? - on his pages, pen in hand. After pausing long enough to splash water on his face and open a soda, the director returned to his story and within minutes was immersed in his characters.

Lucisi entered Michelle's apartment and jokingly whistled again, curious to see if the cat would respond. He chuckled as Sultan came bounding from the back and rubbed against his legs. The detective picked up the cat and scratched him as they crossed to the kitchen where Tom filled the food and water bowls.

While Sultan ate, Lucisi looked around to

confirm that no one had been in the apartment since he left. He also checked the Caller ID display and noted several calls from California phones. That information confirmed for Lucisi what Michelle had believed. The nuisance caller on the West Coast and the intruder at home were not connected.

Having determined that to his satisfaction, Tom ignored the ringing that began as he went back to pet Sultan. Crouching down beside the animal he stroked the silky fur and wished vehemently that Michelle were there to feed her own pet.

"It's not that I mind taking care of you, Cat," he told Sultan as he ran his hand down the Persian's back. "I just want Michelle home again, safe and unharmed."

Sultan gazed up at Tom and purred as if to say, "So do I."

After making sure Sultan was prepared for the night Lucisi drove home and half-heartedly stirred up some supper, wondering if the man who had kidnapped Michelle was feeding her or starving her. The subsequent images of what might be happening to his now-fiancee at the hands of her captor roused such fury in Tom that his hands shook, spilling the seasoning he was sprinkling over the meat. Unproductive thoughts and wild imaginings did not solve cases he told himself and firmly pushed the thoughts from his mind.

His will power was not so strong later when he had gone to bed. Unbidden evil visions filled his mind and ignited his rage. If he did nothing else in his lifetime, he would bring this pervert to justice. In honesty, Lucisi admitted to himself that revenge was more to his taste, but locking a man as obviously warped as the abductor in with some of the felons he had known might prove to be the best revenge of all. Tom smiled grimly at the picture.

Finally, after tossing and turning for over an hour, Lucisi threw back the covers and stalked to the medicine cabinet. He really didn't believe in using chemicals for relaxation but the pills he kept "just in case" had not reached the expiration date on the bottle and Tom knew he needed rest to have his wits about him tomorrow. The pills did their job and before long he was sleeping, though not especially restfully.

CHAPTER 23

It was late afternoon before Michelle's captor paused in his work. He looked at Michelle, who had wormed her way into a position in the corner of the sofa, her back against the arm, her cheek resting on the back. She wasn't comfortable but it was the best she could do with her hands bound behind her.

She jerked as a hand slid gently down her arm. "Oh! You startled me!"

"I didn't mean to scare you."

"Strange words to come from a kidnapper."

"Michelle! How can you say such a thing?" Hurt was obvious in the man's tone. "I love you. I want to be with you all the time." He moved closer to her and kissed her hard while running his hands over her body. Transferring his mouth to her ear he whispered, "I love you so much."

Michelle shivered and wondered how a stranger could have developed this intense passion for her.

"Tell me you love me, too," her captor pleaded.

"I don't know you," she protested.

"You'll love me. I promise. I'll treat you like a queen, much better than that policeman you've been seeing."

"How do you know him?" Michelle demanded sharply, surprised into forgetting her position.

Belatedly it occurred to her abductor that he might have offered a clue to his identity. He was not ready to reveal himself to her yet so he quickly accounted for his comment by saying, "I've watched you with him. I can guess what kind of a man he is."

Michelle, emboldened by her need to defend Tom, retorted, "At least he isn't hiding behind a blindfold and mask."

Her abductor slapped her sharply. Then, overwhelmed by the realization of what he had done, almost cried, "I'm sorry, Michelle. Forgive me , Michelle. I wasn't thinking."

Covering her face and upper body with kisses he murmured over and over, "I'm sorry. I'm sorry. Please forgive me."

The shock of being struck left Michelle speechless. When she regained her composure she took a calculated risk and said stiffly, "I'll forgive you if you'll back off and give me more time to get to know you."

Her tormentor froze in the midst of a wet caress. "Back off?" he croaked harshly. "I'm giving you what women want. How dare you imply that I can't do enough?"

He was gripping her arms tightly and the closeness of his body allowed Michelle to feel his body quiver as rage grew within him. She swallowed and, hating herself for the hypocrisy but feeling no choice, said the words she hoped would deter further abuse.

"Sweetheart, please. Please give me time to become accustomed to you. Please."

The vice-like grip relaxed and his hands slid down toward her wrists, pulling her to him, her face crushed against his chest. She twisted her head to gain more breathing space and the violent pounding of his heart echoed in her ear. His mouth dropped to her neck and moved down to her shoulder in a trail of moist kisses.

Michelle squirmed and gasped, "Please. Let me up. I can't breathe."

The subterfuge worked and her would-be lover released his suffocating hold. Michelle inhaled deeply.

"I'm sorry, darling. I didn't realize I was choking you." He sounded sincerely contrite and it dawned on Michelle that the man was verifiably deranged. This knowledge made her aware that with careful strategy she might be able to manipulate his actions. If she could make him believe that she found him attractive but was not yet ready to be his lover she might get out of this safely. If her compliance was convincing he might be persuaded to lower his guard and increase her opportunities to escape. If. . . If. . . If. . .

"Just give me a minute to catch my breath."

"Of course."

Michelle sat inhaling deeply and frantically playing various lines of approach through her mind.

"It's really uncomfortable, being tied like this. Could you walk me around a little bit?" She looked in what she hoped was the right direction and smiled timidly. Shyness, that would be her first tactic.

With his arm around her waist the kidnapper helped her to her feet and planted a kiss on her cheek. "Certainly, darling. We'll stay inside now but maybe tomorrow we can go outside."

"That would be wonderful." It truly would, but Michelle hoped that her trip outside the next day would be without her captor.

At first Michelle's walk was stilted, her muscles cramped from lack of use and bondage. Still, her body was in good shape and shortly her walk became more normal.

"It feels good to move. I'm used to exercise," she explained.

"I know. I've followed you to your exercise class."

"And everywhere else, so it seems."

"Whenever I could. I know all about you, Michelle. I've studied your movements. Your perfume is as familiar to me as the scent of my aftershave. I buy your brand of toothpaste and your favorite snacks. I could buy your clothes and select the correct sizes and the colors that accent your beauty. I know what you like, what you read, what you watch. Why do you watch those awful Clint Sharkey movies anyway?"

"I find them fascinating. Why do you say they're awful?"

"All of them are so brutal. So many of the characters are perverted."

Michelle fought off the urge to retort, "Perverted! You ought to feel right at home in the middle of one," and instead commented meekly, "I think the complexities of the films make them interesting."

"When we're married we'll have more interesting things to do. You'll see." He squeezed her waist affectionately.

"Have we walked enough, darling. Are you tired?"

"Not a bit," Michelle answered hastily. "I need the exercise. If you're tired you could uncover my eyes and let me continue to pace by myself."

The stratagem failed.

"I can go on for a little longer. Then I have to finish my work."

Michelle was glad to know that her captor had something other than her body to keep him occupied. While he did his preparations she would create plans of her own.

At her request the man agreed to bind Michelle's hands in front but in return for that concession she found herself once again strapped to the bed.

"It's not time for you to remove the blindfold," he told her as he left the bedroom, "and I can't concentrate on my work and watch to see that you're not a naughty, disobedient girl at the same time."

His tone was teasing but Michelle was not amused. The more she stayed in his presence the more she came to understand that, in spite of the constant physical caresses and verbal endearments, this was a man who was contemptuous of women. He was a man to fear and no matter what it took she must find a way to escape his clutches before he perceived her resolve to get away. If he discerned her purpose her life would surely be in danger

Michelle had several plans in mind by the time her abductor came into the bedroom and asked, "Are you hungry? Would you like a sandwich?"

She had no desire for food. Her stomach lurched slightly at the thought of the unpalatable fare he had given her but she replied, "Yes, thank you."

When he returned and sat beside her she struggled to sit up but her bonds were not giving enough.

"I'll help you." The man released the cloths across her waist and ankles but left her hands tied.

"It would be easier for me to eat if my hands were free."

"And also easier for you to unmask your eyes."

"You could become the Ape Man again if you don't trust me but I promise I'll leave the blindfold alone while I eat."

His hesitation was palpable and she thought he was going to refuse. Then he said doubtfully, "Very well. We'll try it. If you make the slightest motion toward the blindfold I'll punish you for breaking your word." He unwrapped the cloth that bound her wrists.

Pandering to his ego Michelle promised submission by throwing back at him his own terminology. "I'll be a good girl. Honest. There'll be no need to punish me."

She rubbed her wrists to make them feel normal and hoped that that her face was not flaming with embarrassment at the blatant blarney she was spouting. Unable to see his face Michelle had only her ears and his touch to cue her to his response.

He took her hands in his and softly kissed the palms before placing a ham sandwich in her grasp. To her surprise the food tasted good and after several bites she requested liquid.

"Is there any tea tonight?"

"Right here ready for you." Her abductor put the glass into her hand.

"Thanks."

"Anything for you, darling."

He sat quietly while she ate, giving her no clue as to his plans for the night. Michelle pondered the best way to bring up the subject. If she could hold off his advances until morning she hoped to be long gone before he returned.

She polished off the last of the sandwich and held out her hand for her glass. "That was good. I hadn't noticed I was hungry."

Michelle's bad choice of words was shown by her captor's next move. He kissed her neck. "Mere food didn't satisfy my hunger." With a lecherous laugh he murmured, "Shall I demonstrate?"

"I think I can guess."

For the first time Michelle's hands were free when he embraced her. She contained her powerful desire to attack him with teeth and fingernails and instead forced herself to reach up and gently stroke the back of his neck.

His reaction shocked her and confirmed her conviction that he was probably certifiably insane. The man burst into tears and clung to her, whispering unintelligible endearments between sobs. Michelle almost panicked and tried to run but, knowing that he was much stronger than she, held fast to her screaming emotions and patted him on the back.

The crying stopped almost as suddenly as it had started. No blindness was enough to prevent Michelle from seeing his intense shame. When he spoke his voice was harsh.

"You shouldn't do things like that to me, Michelle."

Completely taken aback Michelle gasped and pushed away from him. "I thought you wanted me to touch you."

"Not without warning." The stern tone was so

unlike the one he had used earlier Michelle wondered if his mental disorder included multiple personalities. At the same time she became aware that she had heard that severe voice before. It tickled at her mind but she hurriedly thrust the thought to the backburner. At this moment she needed all of her faculties to deal with her abductor's mood swings.

"*You* didn't warn *me.*"

"That's different." He sat on the edge of the bed with his back to her.

"How?"

"You're a woman." His misogyny was showing again.

Michelle decided to try contrition. "I'm sorry."

"It's all right, darling. I forgive you. I understand you were trying to please me."

Michelle strangled back a retort and asked, "Am I not supposed to touch you at all?"

"Oh, yes!" He turned to face her and became quivery again. "Let me show you how."

The man eased beside her on the bed. "Lie down."

Michelle obeyed, fearful of what was coming but more afraid of the consequences of resistance. She felt the warmth of his body pressing close to hers then stifled a scream as he hoisted her up and slid an arm beneath her shoulders.

"Now, put your arms around my neck," he instructed, "and hold me tight."

As she complied he rolled her over and they lay face-to face quietly. To her surprise her captor did not insert the loathsome wet kisses into the embrace nor did he paw at her pajamas. For the moment the contact of their bodies pressed tightly together seemed sufficient for his desires and she felt him relaxing rather than becoming aroused. She gently stroked the back of his head which further soothed him and within minutes she was startled to discover that he had dropped off to sleep.

Michelle considered the possibility of trying to slip away but rejected the idea as unrealistic. The opportunity would be much better after the man left in the morning. She mentally crossed her fingers that he would not wake up with the desire to resume his caresses.

With no clock available Michelle did not know how long her companion slept. She herself drifted in and out of wakefulness further distorting her sense of time but when he stirred murmuring her name it felt like the early hours of the morning. Michelle lay very still in hopes that he would sink back into unconsciousness but to her disappointment he roused, releasing her from his powerful clasp and rolling onto his back.

"You're marvelous, Michelle. I love you very much."

Michelle could not decide on appropriate words to reply and thus remained silent. She, too, shifted her position, aware that it made her more vulnerable but needing to ease her body.

"I guess it's not important, but what time is it?" she queried.

"Time isn't your concern now."

"It's just that I'm used to living by the clock."

"I'll change all that for you. You'll never have to worry about keeping any appointments - except the ones with me."

"Could you humor me and tell me the time now?" Michelle put lightness in her voice.

The man laughed without merriment. "It's three a.m. Does that satisfy you?" From his tone she surmised that her request irritated him.

"Yes, it does. Thank you."

"I'd like to satisfy you in other ways." He reached out to her, running a hand down her throat.

Michelle thought quickly and came up with, "It pleases me to sleep like we did."

"Then I'll please you more." He turned on his side and draped his arm across her. "When I get home tonight we'll be more loving but I need to sleep. I have an important case tomorrow." Her captor squeezed her to him and nestled his face in the crook of her neck.

Michelle forced her body to relax against his but her mind was busy. If he was involved in a case and working on a brief he was surely a member of the legal field. He seemed to have forgotten her unbound hands but she doubted that he would allow her to be free when he left her alone. Somewhere she had heard his voice - the stern, unrelenting one - and once she had it pegged his masquerade was over. Michelle intended to press every charge possible.

Ann Snuggs

CHAPTER 24

The beeping of a watch alarm jerked Michelle awake. Totally disoriented she muttered, "What it is?"

Her captor stirred and pulled his arm free to reach the alarm shut-off.

"I have to leave early this morning, darling. Just lie here until I dress and can fix us some food." He leaned back to kiss her and stiffened. "I forgot your hands." Fumbling around he located a strip of cloth and rapidly bound her wrists.

Disappointment swept Michelle. She had hoped he would neglect her bonds. She flounced on the bed and took heart upon the realization that he had not taken time to tie her down.

Michelle rolled to her side and eased her

hands toward her face. She tested the edge of the blindfold. Yes! The cloth had stretched enough that it gave with little resistance as she tugged at it.

Listening carefully she heard the sound of the shower then the water shutting off. Michelle peeked cautiously from under the blindfold. The bathroom door was open and she could clearly see within. The figure of a man emerged from the shower and reached for a towel. She observed him drape the towel over a rod and turn to the lavatory to shave.

When the light at the mirror hit him full in the face she stifled a gasp. Definitely this man knew the law. The reflection in the mirror was plainly Eric Pedersen, the deputy prosecutor who had believed she would be an excellent witness. How could she have failed to recognize him at Martinelli's that Saturday? She resolved to be an excellent witness in this case, too, and hoped her testimony would be sufficient to bury him under the jail. Kidnapping was a serious crime.

Having learned the identity of her tormentor, Michelle adjusted the blindfold to its former position. It would be dangerous, maybe fatal, for her abductor to have any hint of her newly gained knowledge.

It took all of Michelle's acting skills to carry out her part of Pedersen's morning plans. She cooperated in every way until he prepared to leave.

"Please, sw - sw- sweetheart." She stammered on the endearment. "I know you can get into my apartment. Could you please bring me some things when you come back? It would mean a lot to me to have my favorite sweats and a change of underwear. Please." Michelle made her voice soft and pleading. "Please."

The idea of handling Michelle's clothing, especially her undergarments, appealed strongly to the attorney. He also liked the domestic sound of bringing things home to his woman at the end of the day.

"I'll see what I can do." He sat beside her and stroked his hands on her body. "I hate to leave you alone like this."

An inspiration flashed into Michelle's mind. "It will be a long day. I'll miss you." Like fun, she added to herself.

He bent to administer a final deep, searching kiss.

"Oh, please let me up for one last time in the bathroom before you go. You'll be gone so long."

"I'm late now."

"Please. I'll hurry."

"All right," he consented reluctantly, and began to untie the cloths.

After her captor had left in what sounded to Michelle like a cloud of dust and burning rubber, she checked her bonds. To her delight the improvised trick had worked. In his haste to get away her captor had done an inadequate job of retying the restraining cloths. Michelle was sure that within the hour she could release them.

The task was more difficult than she had expected. The strip across her ankles loosened easily enough and her legs were soon free, but the one that held her arms down at her waist was more firmly knotted. She tried ooching toward the foot of the bed but her breasts would not fit beneath the binding cloth. After struggling for what seemed like hours, but was only minutes, she wiggled the other direction and attempted to roll over under the restraint but accomplished nothing more than an abrasion on her arm where skin and bond fought against each other and the cloth won.

Michelle lay still for a moment, puffing. She considered screaming to see if anyone might hear her, but the fact that her kidnapper had left her ungagged meant that he had imprisoned her a distance from other people. It would be wiser to save her breath. She might as well take account of her options while she took a break.

In the lull following her activity Michelle almost dropped off to sleep. She yanked herself back from half-consciousness sternly, aware that before Pederson returned she had to be long gone and finding the way out of this place could be very time-consuming.

If she couldn't move to the foot of the bed maybe she could go to the headboard. Michelle used her feet to push upward. Once again the restraint scraped at the skin on her arms - how could cloth be so harsh? - but gradually she worked her way upward and after what seemed an eternity of hurt she managed to pull her bound wrists out of the strap which pinned her to the bed.

"Thank goodness!" she said with a loud sigh of relief. Michelle stretched her arms and pushed the blindfold from her eyes. She lay without moving, blinking and exercising her eyes to adjust to the light. Never again would she take the sense of sight for granted.

Before long her vision became more normal and she sat up. With her arms no longer beneath the binding which had pinned her to the bed there was plenty of slack and Michelle easily wriggled out from under it. Now only the cloth around her wrists remained.

Michelle crossed to the door and looked at the part of her prison she had not seen. The entire structure consisted of but three rooms, plus the obviously added bath. She stepped into a living-dining area and then peered into a messy kitchen. Pedersen was certainly unskilled at household chores, she reflected.

She entered the kitchen and inspected the counter. No knife there. Maybe the drawers. Every kitchen needed a knife. At last her quest was rewarded. The third drawer she opened held three knives. Michelle selected one and cut at the cloth gingerly. It took some effort and contortions but finally the cloth was down to a few threads which she snapped with a quick jerk. Blood oozed from several nicks but essentially her wrists were unharmed.

Her survey of the place showed no telephone so she would have to walk out. As her abductor had brought none of her shoes, probably on purpose, that would not be fun, especially if she was far enough from civilization not to warrant a gag. She prowled around to see if any type of footwear was in evidence but her search was for naught.

Clearly her kidnapper had prepared this place simply to confine her. Nothing of his had been housed here and only the meagerest of furnishings occupied the rooms.

Michelle had her choice of two doors and chose the one in the kitchen. She eased the door open and peeked out. The structure stood in a wooded area with trees practically on the doorstep. The sounds that greeted her ears were those of a forest. Not even the distant noise of traffic could be distinguished.

She pulled back in and went to the other door. Michelle had definitely heard her captor drive away so some type of road reached the house.

The front opened onto a narrow, ill-kept driveway. Two ruts with tufts of grass in between led from an area of weeds where the car had been parked around a bend in the trees. Well, standing here was a waste of time, and time was not her friend right now.

Michelle slipped out, her eyes darting in all directions, as she warily moved onto the rutted path. The dust was soft between her toes. When she turned the bend more trees came into view. The driveway seemed to stretch forever.

The sun was almost directly overhead and Michelle was acutely aware of the passage of time as she rounded the fourth turn in the path which abruptly ended at an asphalt road. She jumped back when a car roared down the paved highway right in front of her, the driver never even looking back.

Michelle looked up and down the highway trying to decide which way to travel. She had no idea where she was or how far the nearest town might be located. The urgency of finding help soon bore down upon her making her oblivious to the discomfort of her bare feet on the pavement. She flipped a coin mentally and turned left.

For the better part of an hour Michelle walked without meeting any sign of life. Then two cars passed her within five minutes of each other but neither stopped or slowed for the bedraggled figure trudging along the side of the road. She began to feel dizzy from the cumulative hardships of her exertions of the morning coupled with two days of incarceration.

Michelle contemplated sitting to rest but was afraid to pause with time hounding her. She continued to plod on, fighting weariness that grew with every step. It became harder and harder to keep putting one foot in front of the other and she was practically staggering when she saw a county sheriff's car coming toward her.

As it neared her Michelle waved and the car slowed. She stopped and waited for it to come even with her position. The young officer inside scrutinized her, taking in her unsteadiness and disheveled appearance, then pulled the car to the shoulder of the road. She turned and stumbled toward the vehicle.

"Isn't it pretty early for you to be in this condition, lady?" the young man chided. "I'm afraid

I'm going to have to take you in."

Michelle looked at him blankly. "Please take me to a phone. I have to call my boyfriend - I mean fiance."

"Were you out here drinking together?"

Michelle recoiled from the question and, using most of her reserve strength, drew herself up straight.

"I haven't been drinking. I was kidnapped!"

The young deputy regarded her skeptically. "Right." He reached for his handcuffs.

"No." Michelle backed away and, to her horror, felt tears begin to start. "I've been tied up since Friday night. You're no better than that nutcase that kidnapped me. Please take me to a phone."

Doubt flicked across the officer's face. No odor of liquor was evident and the panic in Michelle's eyes seemed to be genuine. He took a step toward her. She flinched away and lost her balance.

Too weak to regain control and remain standing Michelle fell on the grass beside the car. The deputy stretched out a hand to help her up but she feebly slapped it aside and torturously crawled to her knees and pushed herself up. She stood there reeling and in a pleading tone repeated her request.

"Please take me to a phone."

"Okay, lady." He offered his hand again. "Let me help you and we'll go back to the office."

Michelle allowed him to support her arm and slumped into the back seat of the patrol car. Sitting after so much time on her feet felt wonderful despite the circumstances.

The officer got into the driver's seat and reached for the radio.

"Jackie," he said when the dispatcher responded, "I'm out here on eighty-five and I've got a woman in my car who says she's been kidnapped. She appears to be under the influence of something and I'm coming in with her."

Michelle could not distinguish Jackie's words but from the young man's reaction she surmised that Tom had wasted little time in starting a search for her.

The deputy turned to her. "What's your name?" he asked.

"Michelle Wilson."

His voice sounded less official and more sympathetic. "Don't you worry about a thing, Ms. Wilson. We'll be back to the office in no time and get you whatever you need."

He whipped the car around in a sharp U-turn and accelerated, giving no thought to the speed limit.

Soon Michelle found herself in a county sheriff's office located in a small community some thirty-five miles from the city. Now that she had been identified as a victim rather than a criminal the officer was kindness itself. Jackie turned out to be a woman just a size larger than Michelle and she graciously offered to take Michelle to her home - which was a short two streets away - and allow her to shower and change into some fresh clothes.

The sheriff had notified Lucisi of Michelle's escape by the time she arrived at the office. Knowing that he was on the way to get her, Michelle gratefully accepted Jackie's proposal and before Tom reached the small town she was refreshed and becoming impatient.

When he entered the office she sprang up from her chair and flung herself into his arms. He drew her tenderly to his chest and stroked her hair lightly. The touch of his strong, protective caresses undid Michelle and she began to cry quietly. Her body heaved within his embrace but she made no sound.

"It's all right. It's all right," Tom said softly. "I'm going to take care of everything. Don't worry." He continued to stand and hold her against him until her sobs ceased and she released her tenacious grip and stepped back, still clinging to his hand.

"I'm so embarrassed," she murmured, covering her tear-stained face with her free hand. "I can't believe I went to pieces like that."

"It's a normal reaction," Tom assured her.

At the same time Jackie said, "With all you've been through you'd be strange if you didn't cry a little."

Michelle smiled weakly. "Thanks."

Now that his fiancee was safe and calm Lucisi unloosened her hold on his fingers and sat down with the sheriff to transact business. After a few minutes he glanced at Michelle and gestured for her to join them.

"Do you think you can find the place where

you were held?"

Michelle raised a shoulder indicating doubt. "Maybe. With enough time, but I need to show you something vitally important at my apartment. It will explain a lot and is much more urgent than locating the house in the woods right now." She threw him a pleading look.

Lucisi read her eyes and turned to the sheriff. "Could you help us search tomorrow? Or just have Deputy Rogers here show me where he picked up Michelle. I can take it from there and I want to see the clue she's talking about as soon as possible."

The sheriff nodded. "Whatever you think is best, detective. We want to cooperate on a crime like this. My own daughter is around Ms. Wilson's age and I'd sure be hot to have every bit of help available if she were in that situation."

"Then I'll give you a call tomorrow." Tom shook hands with the sheriff. "Thanks a lot."

Ann Snuggs

CHAPTER 25

Michelle said good-byes and thanks all around and she and Tom went to his car. She sat silently while he braked for the one stop light in town and increased his speed as they reached the open highway.

Lucisi stretched over and patted her hand. "Michelle, you don't know how very thankful I am to see you alive and safe." He brushed his fingers across the abrasion on her arm. "Did he do that to you?" Controlled rage vibrated in his voice. "If I wasn't sworn to uphold the law I'd take it into my own hands when we find him."

Michelle clutched the out-stretched fingers with her own. "I was terrified, Tom. He intended to keep me prisoner forever."

"What's at your apartment? You sounded like you didn't want to talk about it at the sheriff's office."

"There's nothing at my apartment. I needed to be alone with you. Tom, I know who was stalking me. I *know* the kidnapper. And so do you."

Lucisi turned to look at her so abruptly that the car swerved on the road.

"*I* do!" he exclaimed. "Who is it?"

"Do you remember me telling you about being a witness in a robbery trial?"

"Yeah."

"And I said the deputy prosecuting attorney chose me because he believed I'd be a credible witness?"

Tom nodded and commented, "Police work has developed my patience but I think you're building the suspense more than necessary."

"I didn't realize that's what I was doing. The bottom line is that Mr. Prosecutor believed I'd be a credible object of his affections, too. Eric Pedersen is the one who's been stalking me and the one who kidnapped me Friday night."

Lucisi stared at her in amazement. "I can't believe it!"

"Well, it's true," Michelle snapped defensively.

"I wasn't doubting you," Tom hastily reassured her. "It's that he has a reputation for being so involved in his work. He never socializes at all. I told you someone would probably have to identify him for me in a crowd and . . . ." His voice trailed off.

"That's the key, isn't it? No social life at all and after he watched you testify you became his obsession."

"Something like that. I've had plenty of time to think this weekend, lying there tied up and blindfolded." She shuddered and tears once again welled up in her eyes. Noticing them, Tom pulled to the side of the highway and took her in his arms.

Michelle buried her face in his chest and sobbed, this time aloud. She clung to Tom as if her life depended on the hold. The warmth of his encircling arms comforted her and gradually her crying slackened. She began to breathe deeply, working to regain her composure.

"We don't have time for this," she gasped chokingly. "I need to have a warrant sworn out."

"I can take care of it."

"You don't understand. He's going to my apartment before he leaves the city tonight. You can arrest him there."

"Why would he return to the scene of the crime, so to speak?"

"Because this morning I played up to him and he promised to bring me some of my things from home. Please, Tom. I want him under lock and key as quickly as possible."

"You thought this out pretty well, didn't you?"

"I tried hard. I really did. And I had lots of time."

Lucisi slid back under the wheel. "Okay, master strategist," his voice was warm and affectionate, "let's see if we can put your plan into action."

All was quiet inside the car for miles and they were at the outskirts of the city when Michelle said softly, "I didn't make love with him, Tom, if that's what you're wondering."

Lucisi flicked a glance in her direction. "Does that mean he raped you?" His voice was purposefully toneless and objective.

"No. He was awful weird. He kept running his hands up and down my body but he never tried to strip off my pajamas."

Tom's peripheral vision told him that Michelle was sitting stiffly against the seat reciting the words as if by rote, hoping to purge the memory from her mind.

"His kisses were a nightmare, wet and yucky. Is it all right for me to say this to you, Tom? I need to get it out."

Lucisi gently rubbed her shoulder. "You say whatever you need to say. I love you and am going to marry you. You can tell me anything you want - or need to."

Michelle took his hand and held it against her cheek. "Tom, I love you, too. When you asked me to marry you I wasn't really sure. Now I am."

The detective smiled broadly, the first genuine smile Michelle had seen since he picked her up.

"You can't imagine how glad I am to hear that. I was afraid that this experience might make you reluctant to have a man near you. I've seen victims react that way."

In spite of the traffic, Michelle unfastened her seatbelt and slid across the seat to cuddle close to Tom. "Not you. You're special. Every time Pedersen touched me I'd hate him more because it wasn't your touch. I hated him intensely because he kept me from being with you."

"You said you were blindfolded. How did you find out his identity?"

"I didn't until today. This morning he was careless and tied my hands together but not down. I pushed the blindfold up and saw him in the mirror while he was shaving."

"Does he know you know who he is?"

"No. I'm sure he would have tied me more securely had he known."

They had almost reached the police station when Michelle stated firmly, "I intend to be there when you arrest him at my apartment."

Tom glanced at her with a look of exasperation. "Michelle, be reasonable. He may be dangerous. He probably carries a gun. It would be easy enough for him to get a permit."

Michelle waited until Tom had parked the car then reached up with both hands and turned his face to hers. Gazing directly into his eyes she spoke steadily and resolutely.

"I have to be there, Tom. It's necessary for me to put this behind me. If you insist on going alone that faint barrier will always be between us."

"I won't go alone. Mike will go with me."

"That's not the point. I have to go, too."

"We'll see," Tom stalled.

Michelle was pleasantly surprised to discover just how much having a policeman personally involved speeded up the procedure and, in spite of her concern, they arrived at her apartment well before the case her abductor was prosecuting recessed for the day.

No amount of opposition from Tom had prevented her from going with the detectives. No matter what tact Lucisi had tried she had sturdily stated, "I have to be there," until finally Fitzgerald had declared in exasperation, "For Pete's sake, Tom! Nothing you say can dissuade her. Let her go."

When Lucisi opened the door he whistled and to Michelle's amazement Sultan bounced into the living room and rubbed against the detective's legs. She stared at the two of them in wonder.

"What is this?" she exclaimed. "When I was grabbed Sultan wasn't even speaking to you!"

"I've been taking care of him. Angie wanted to do it but I didn't want her coming in and walking into your admirer."

Sultan transferred his affection to Michelle who picked him up and nestled her face in his fur. The cat purred loudly.

"All this good feeling is terrific," commented Lucisi's partner, "but don't you think we ought to decide positioning and be ready in case Pedersen arrives earlier than we've calculated?"

"You're right." Tom became all business. "Michelle, go into another room, get settled and stay there quietly. Don't do anything and especially don't say anything. You might speak just as he opens the door and we want him inside. Do you understand?" He looked directly into her eyes.

"Yes, and I'll do exactly what you tell me. I know you didn't want me to come and I appreciate the concession." She disappeared through the doorway.

Lucisi and Fitzgerald glanced around the living room and Fitzgerald said, "Your lady's plan to contain him in this room was a good one. Once he steps inside and closes the door he'll be trapped. Why don't I wait behind that table by the door and block him in as soon as he enters? You could crouch between those chairs against the wall and make the arrest."

"Sounds good to me. Let's do it."

Footsteps echoed on the sidewalk and the detectives hurried their prearranged positions. Tom was barely in place when the key turned in the lock.

Pedersen entered with the manner of one who belongs and pushed the door shut behind him. The late evening light was sufficient and he started across the room without switching on a lamp. When he was even with the coffee table, Lucisi rose and stated firmly, "Freeze, Pedersen, you're under arrest."

Without hesitation the prosecutor whirled to run for the door but found his way blocked by Fitzgerald. His hand darted under his coat and Tom drew his revolver. Pedersen did not complete his original action but flung himself at Lucisi, reaching for the gun.

Tom attempted to side-step and avoid the

lunge but the attorney managed to grasp his gun hand and the two of them went down in a heap. Fitzgerald crossed toward them but his legs were cut from under him by a flailing kick as he reached the struggle.

At the sound of Tom's voice Michelle had crept to the doorway desiring to confront her captor once he was in custody and she stared in dismay at the bodies tangled in combat.

Both men clung tightly to the gun, each trying to wrest it from the other's grasp, but their strengths were evenly matched. Neither could overpower the other.

Michelle winced and cried out as a shot fired and Tom collapsed atop the prosecutor. Without thought for consequences she dashed to him and cried, "Tom. Tom."

Lucisi pushed himself up and off of the body of the warped deputy prosecutor and embraced Michelle, wiping tears from her cheeks.

"It's all right, *carissima*. It's all over." They knelt by the body with her face against his blood-stained shirt while he rocked her gently, stroking her hair and whispering words of love and comfort.

Mike clapped a hand on Tom's shoulder and the lovers looked up. "That was close," Fitzgerald commented. "Glad to see you came out on top."

"That makes two of us." Lucisi grinned.

"Three of us," added Michelle. "Can we count on you to be at our wedding?" she asked Tom's partner.

"At it?" Tom snorted. "He'll be in it."

"I'll call for the coroner." Mike left them together and went to the phone.

Clint and Pete sat together in their favorite trendy restaurant, each glowing with success. They toasted each other for the fourth time and ordered another round.

"Wait until you see me in this performance," Pete told his friend boastfully. "I don't usually brag on myself but you'll be impressed. You never dreamed I had it in me."

"I'll look forward to it. I've always thought you were talented," Clint responded magnanimously. "If you can come across vicious enough maybe there'll be a plum part for you in my upcoming project."

"Is this the screenplay you were writing when I left."

"Uh-uh. You wait till you read this one. I was totally inspired. Never wrote anything so quickly and probably never will again. Remember when you called last week I told you about the bitch who answered Michelle's phone?"

"Yeah."

"Well, when I thought about a woman I was calling being stalked by a man there in her home town the whole film flashed through my brain so fast that I could hardly get it down."

"You've already pitched it and found a backer?"

"Frigging right! Of course my story line

focuses on two stalkers, both deranged, who end up confronting each other over the woman they both want. The female is incidental, but I have to admit none of it would've come to me without Michelle."

"So what are you doing to show appreciation?"

"It's enough for her to have the privilege of inspiring me, Clint Sharkey, with a box office hit, because take my word on it, this one will me a big grosser."

"And she'll just happen to know she's your inspiration?"

Clint shook his head, a little sadly. "No. Not knowing what action she might take I can't afford to divulge my identity, but I'm going to leave her alone after one last call."

"I'm glad to hear that, for your sake more than hers. When will you make it?"

"Tonight, if she's home. I haven't been able to reach her all week."

Pete held up his glass and Clint touched his to it.

"Here's to the last call," said Pete.

Friday afternoon Michelle was at last allowed to return to her apartment after spending the week with Angie. She released Sultan, who strolled around sniffing at the interesting smells left by the assortment of people who had passed through in his absence.

Michelle felt compelled to clean even though

a cleaning service had been called in while she was gone. For the third time she was vacuuming the rug where the body of her stalker had rested when the doorbell rang. A glance through the peephole showed her fiance at the door with a sack from KFC in hand.

She let him in and looked questioningly at his offering.

He grinned cheerfully. "Once upon a time you said meals at your place were likely to be KFC so I obliged."

"Great!" Michelle stretched up to kiss him. "Sit down and rest. I'll get plates and something to drink."

Sultan bounced past her and sprang into Tom's lap. Michelle shook her head and called back from the kitchen, "I'll never understand how you taught him to do that."

"Talent," Lucisi responded confidently, then laughed. "In some past life I must have been a circus animal trainer."

They spent the evening quietly cuddled in each others arms, making plans for their future together.

Michelle was curled contentedly in bed drifting off into dreams of Tom when the phone jerked her wide awake. She checked the ID. Sure enough, her caller from California. Ignoring the ring, she rolled back over then remembered that, intentionally or not, he had tipped them off to the threat here. She reached for the phone.

"Hello."

"Michelle! At last! Where have you been?" The caller sounded delighted.

Deciding to try bluntness Michelle said, "Kidnapped."

"No shit?"

"That's the truth. The only reason I answered your call just now was because if you hadn't started calling me when you did, I would not have known someone was after me until he snatched me. I owe you for that."

"Glad I could help," Clint replied smoothly, then added, "Are you all right?"

"Not that I'm sure you care, but yes, I'm fine, and I'm also engaged to the detective you unwittingly brought into my life. I owe you for that, too."

Clint laughed suggestively. "My pleasure. I'm giving you another gift tonight. This is my last call. You've been a great inspiration to me. You might say we've been lucky for each other."

"I'm glad I could help you, too. Won't you tell me who you are?"

"You're a lot smarter than I thought you'd be when I first read your letter. Maybe you can figure it out. Good-bye, Michelle. See you at the movies."

Michelle heard a soft click on the line and replaced her receiver. She felt an odd sensation of loss knowing that he would not call again, for her sixth sense told her that he had been telling the truth. What a strange parting statement. "See you at the movies." Oh, well. She had more delectable things to think on. Michelle soon slipped into a happy dream of Tom.

Ann Snuggs

EPILOGUE

Michelle had taken the week off to prepare for hers and Tom's Saturday wedding. To her delight Angie had taken some time off, too. Thursday afternoon saw them packing things at Michelle's for Tom to take to his place after work.

"I picked up the new *Hollywood Lives* yesterday. There's a big article about Clint Sharkey's new film coming out next week. Would you like to read it? The movie is expected to be a box office smash."

"Yeah. What's it about?"

"You might want to skip the movie. It's about two men stalking the same woman. It might bring up some unpleasant memories."

"Oh, Angie! All that was months ago. The

weirdo didn't really hurt me and he certainly won't reappear. Being with Tom has been all the therapy I'll ever need. It might be interesting to see how Sharkey handles the idea."

Just then the doorbell rang. Angie hopped up and went to the door and returned shortly with a elaborate bouquet of yellow roses.

"Tom really got carried away," she remarked.

Michelle looked at the roses speculatively. "My traditional Tom usually sends red - or pink if the florist doesn't have enough red."

She pulled the card from the pick and pulled it from the envelop. After a glance at it she silently handed it to Angie, who gasped when she saw it.

The card read, "Thanks for the inspiration. Someone."

Double Stalk

ABOUT THE AUTHOR

    Ann Snuggs created stories before she could write, telling them to her mother to be written down. She has worked as a newspaper copy editor, columnist and feature writer; taught a variety of subjects and levels in public schools; and generally describes herself as a Jill-of-All-Trades.

    Ann writes what she likes to read - short, character-driven stories, no matter what the genre.

    In addition to *Double Stalk,* she has written two books on Western movies, *Riding the (Silver Screen) Range* and *Uncredited: Cliff Lyons, On and Off Screen;* and one Western novel, *Donovan's Trail*. She also contributed two selections to the anthology, *Tales From the South, Volume 1*.

Made in the USA
Charleston, SC
31 October 2016